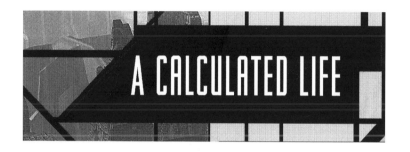

Anne Charnock

47NORTH

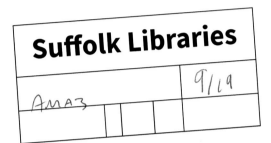

The characters and events portrayed in this book are fictitious. Any similarity to real persons, living or dead, is coincidental and not intended by the author.

Printed in the United States of America.

Published by 47North, Seattle
www.apub.com

ISBN-13: 9781477849514
ISBN-10: 1477849513

Cover by *the*Book Designers

Library of Congress Control Number: 2013945044

For Garry, Adam, and Robert

But a thought swarmed in me; what if he, this yellow-eyed being—in his ridiculous, dirty bundle of trees, in his uncalculated life—is happier than us?

We—Yevgeny Zamyatin

A CALCULATED LIFE

CHAPTER 1

The second-smallest stick insect lay askew and lifeless on the trails of ivy. Jayna lifted the mesh cover, nudged the foliage with her middle finger, and the corpse dropped to the cage floor. It made no sense. The smallest of the brood, the outlier, should have died first. Why this one, the second smallest? She glanced at the temperature monitor. Surely, it wasn't her fault? And it couldn't be the food—she turned over a leaf—or they would all be ill by now. So what exactly…? The surviving insects shuddered indifferently.

Jayna placed the cover back on its base. One thing was certain. An autopsy was out of the question; she had no scalpels. In any case, she thought, it was a fact: in the normal run of things, people had autopsies; insects did not. She pushed a hand through her hair. One dead stick insect and now she was running two minutes late for breakfast. That's all the death amounted to—a slight delay in her morning routine. The death would remain a mystery. No ripple of concern, no cascade of grief. She peered into the cage at the still-smallest stick insect.

"Maybe you're…just lucky," she murmured.

———

Jayna left Rest Station C7 with her friend Julie and together they headed towards the tower blocks of downtown Manchester. They looked like schoolgirls, holding their packed lunches and wearing identical office garb.

"Why would the smallest, feeblest one survive longer?" said Jayna.

"Was it feeble? Perhaps it was just…small," said Julie.

By the time they reached the Vimto sculpture on Granby Row, Jayna had scanned through the data she'd compiled over the past three months on the eating habits of her stick insects, their rates of growth, their response to stimuli—light, heat, and touch—morning and evening activity rates…thirteen variables in all. She plotted against time, overlaid the graphs, and compared. No help at all.

"I kept a close eye on them all but I only took measurements for two—the two closest to average size," said Jayna.

"Hmm. Mistake."

The morning street projections let rip with the usual inducements—half-price breakfast deals, lunchtime soup 'n' sushi specials. Julie peeled off northwards. Jayna, still perplexed, pressed ahead and pulled up sixteen data sets culled over recent weeks from a slew of enthusiasts' forums and from academic studies by the Bangalore Environmental Research Institute. Rates of growth, population size, mortality figures; it was all there. She plotted the longevity of stick insects against their size at death, and regressed the data. The correlation with size was…heck, weaker than she'd imagined. She tripped on a raised paving flag. And as for *luck*, she thought, the tiniest survivor in mind, that was without doubt a dumbed-down term referring to randomness.

On entering the high atrium of the Grace Hopper Building, she walked under the turquoise-leaved palms and bit her lip. She pushed the Bangalore data from her mind and considered her Monday schedule as she stepped to the back of the elevator. The doors closed with a *whoosh-chang!* and she tapped the back of her head against the elevator panel.

Time to think straight. How should she handle her entrance? Act as though nothing had happened on Friday? Walk straight past Eloise? Or should she apologize without any delay? It was just too awkward…and confusing. She hoped Eloise had calmed down over the weekend. According to Benjamin, it was a simple misjudgment. "A minor faux pas"—his exact words. The elevator doors opened and she stepped out. She was relieved Benjamin had said *minor*. A *bit* of a faux pas would be worse, definitely.

Pushing open the office door, she came to a decision. She would keep quiet, hope for the best.

Eloise jumped up, lifted a hand—not exactly a wave—and scuffled across the analysts' floor at Mayhew McCline to intercept Jayna. "Tea!" she said, and pulled Jayna towards the kitchen galley. "Listen, I'm sorry about Friday."

"No. I'm the one who's sorry, Eloise. How was your father?"

"You were right. No real panic. He was comfortable and sedated when I got there."

"You were worried. I wasn't—"

"I overreacted. I didn't mean it."

"Is he still in hospital?"

"Yes, should be home tomorrow." She cocked her head to one side. "It was a very nasty fall, you know…but nothing's broken. They're running tests, giving him a full check."

"That's—"

"I shouldn't have barked at you."

Jayna raised her eyebrows fractionally. She didn't disagree. What had she said that was so bad? "Don't forget the monthly figures before you go. Only take a minute." It hadn't exactly been a quarrel; too brief and one-sided. Jayna reassessed the incident: Eloise pushing things into her bag, one arm in her coat. She'd barged past and *barked* so the whole department heard, "You really are *the bloody limit*, Jayna." The emphasis still caught her by surprise. And then Eloise had thrown open the office door. Her coat belt got caught on the handle. She'd yanked at the belt and shoved the door, which had slammed back against the wall.

"Darjeeling, black, isn't it?" Eloise turned and hit the kettle switch. "Jayna, you have to understand. We can't all be as calm as you."

Jayna shook her head, "Nothing for me, thanks," and turned to leave but Eloise touched her arm. "Listen, to be honest, I wanted to clear the air quickly. Something serious…" She hesitated. "You'd better see Benjamin, now. It's about Tom Blenkinsop." Eloise frowned at Jayna's blankness and, as if spelling things out for a child, "It's…not…good."

——

A bugbear, that Tom. She should have told him; if he needed so much help he should have asked through proper channels, booked some extra training, some official mentoring time. Maybe Benjamin had found out about his off-loading. It had started two months back when Tom sent her a research report before submitting it to Benjamin, with a request: *Cast an eye over this, will you, Jayna?* An aberration; an extra step in the accredited process. On the first three occasions the amendments had taken less than ten minutes but, from that point on, Tom's requests had landed every few days and the reports had become weightier. She hadn't complained because once she'd corrected the first report she hadn't liked the idea of Tom's errors reaching Benjamin. He might have missed them. So Jayna had developed the habit of charging the time to her own jobs; five minutes here, ten minutes there. She finessed his arguments, improved his executive summaries—his weakest area—and, when essential, she hunted down additional data sources to "beef things up," as Tom himself would say.

Benjamin usually worked in the middle of the analysts' floor on the thirty-first but this morning he summoned staff to the thirty-second, to his so-called quiet room.

"About Tom?" she said, poking her head around his door. Benjamin, slumped in his sofa, looked up at Jayna and seemingly had no inclination to say anything. She felt hot. "I thought his last report—"

"It's not about his work," he said, and gestured to the armchair.

"You know he's…he was on holiday?"

She did. Tom had dropped another tome on her before he left, with a brief note: *Check and forward. Thx.*

"*Was* on holiday?"

"Tragic accident," he said. "I want to tell everyone individually."

"Tragic?"

"Swimming in the sea…"

Benjamin, she realized, had already told the story several times. He didn't continue. So she prompted: "Drowned?"

"His wife and kids were on the beach. Couldn't do anything about it."

"That's terrible."

"Swept out. His brother phoned me last night at home. He's flying out today."

Another silence. What was she supposed to say? She recalled a drowning incident reported in the news. What did the journalist ask…?

"Have they found his body?" she said with precision.

"No. Not yet. Only happened yesterday."

"That's terrible."

"And it's going to be a long time before there's a funeral. There'll be an autopsy when they find the body…"

Stumped.

"Jayna, can you help me out?" Benjamin, gray-faced, pulled himself up to sit straight-backed. Was this one problem too many for Benjamin, she wondered, or was he upset? Tom had only joined seven months ago. "Can you go through his files? Finish anything that needs finishing. I think the others might find it too upsetting, so soon."

"Okay. I'm familiar—"

"Thanks. Don't tell the others. Just fit it around your own work. Let me know if I need to do any firefighting."

A secondary post-mortem, she thought. "Fine."

———

Jayna stepped along the corridor's repeat-pattern squares and dipped into the washroom. Inside the end cubicle, she leaned back against the door.

Such bad timing! Rebuffing Tom…of all the opportunities I could have taken, Jayna reproached herself. *He didn't bother to explain… just assumed.* She flushed the toilet unnecessarily as though eradicating her response to his request: *Tom, I can't possibly find time until the end of the month. Send it to Benjamin, as is.* He'd retorted: *FU2. Thanks for nothing, wonder woman.*

I didn't know he was in a rush, going on holiday. How stupid of him to drown!

What, she wondered, were the chances of Tom's death? In the entire working population of the Grace Hopper Building she'd expect a premature fatality…once a year? But at Mayhew McCline, with only forty-five employees, the chance of anyone drowning was so small it was technically…She stopped herself and opened the door.

It was never negligible, it was always there. She turned the tap, too far, and water shot out from the basin. Accidents simply happened.

———

The kitchen became the unofficial, designated space for commiserations and the occasional sobbing over Tom as though the analysts were protecting their office space from permanent stains of association. Jayna observed Eloise zigzagging through the department with a condolence card. She averted her eyes as each person hesitated with pen poised. Eloise didn't bring the card to Jayna.

Hester, chief analyst, announced she was installing herself for the morning in Benjamin's quiet room and they all knew what she'd be doing—she'd inform colleagues in London about Tom's death and speak to his personal business contacts, get them reassigned to other analysts. Jayna imagined ripples of concern of varying magnitude spreading from all these subsidiary nodes. No such after-effects from her stick insect's demise.

She brought up Tom's files on her array. And immediately closed them. Instead, she pulled up her own studies and began drilling through her energy data sets. Hydrogen, she decided, was worth a closer look. She interrogated the data on hydrogen car ownership, rotated the charts and geographical visuals—global, continental, and regional—and calculated a trend for global hydrogen car ownership over the past five-years. Next, she searched for a correlation with individual variables in other data sets: disposable income for the same period, fresh fruit exports, per capita holiday spending, a host of commodity production figures, wholesale energy prices…thirty-seven variables in all. Her array flashed, cycling through regressions and wildly fluctuating figures for statistical significance. She brushed twenty-one possibilities aside. Playing with combinations of the remaining variables, she derived seventeen relationships. A fair start, she thought. By instinct, she assigned a weighting for each variable and began her quest for the perfect curve, one that matched the five-year historical trend. And as she adjusted the weightings, the curves began their shape shifting. Benjamin appeared at Jayna's shoulder. "How can you take it all in? I feel sick just watching."

But Jayna refused the interruption. She was closing in but the match simply wasn't good enough. There was nothing to flag up, as yet, for Benjamin. Definitely needed more variables. She could, at this stage, submit a bland sector summary on hydrogen, but anyone could do that. No, she wanted nothing less than a full investment strategy. Worth spending the extra time. She checked her own performance statistics. On average, over her six months' service to date, she'd concluded three projects a week, quadruple the frequency of anyone else in the department. Yes, she could afford to spend more time on hydrogen.

———

Sitting in the park, as she always did after work on Monday, she threw crumbs to her left and right and occasionally ahead of her. Such simple creatures. Each time she flicked her wrist, she reckoned only one or two pigeons espied the flight of stale scraps. She tested her theory by throwing crumbs to her far right. One pigeon twisted around, reacting in the instant. Correct. The other pigeons followed as though a switch had been thrown in each of their tiny brains. Jayna threw to the far left. Again, a single cadger tracked the new trajectory. Leading one minute, subservient the next.

Bother! Maybe she should have rewritten Tom's report. She shook out the remaining crumbs from her paper bag. But she'd been right to consider her own productivity. It was all getting way out of hand. *I know now what I should have done.* She flattened the paper bag against her thigh and made quarter folds. *From the outset I should have allocated the time I spent on his jobs to* his *timesheet, not mine, without asking him. He'd have thought twice, then, about asking for help.*

The birds were in a frenzy. Their heads jabbed, jabbing the air as they jerked along, jabbing at the crumbs on the ground. Jayna examined the evidence of their mishaps—empty eye sockets, stump feet, trailing feathers—and noticed that two of the birds were verging on obese.

And as for Eloise and her father, she rolled her eyes to the treetops, *I still get it wrong.*

———

On the way to her residence in Granby Row, she stopped by the garish menu boards at the Jasmin Five Star Tandoori Restaurant and examined the names of the dishes: King Prawn Vindaloo, Aloo Methi, Bindi Bhaji, Baroa Mozaa. A waiter hovered in the doorway, so she turned away before he could begin his entreaties. No point wasting his time. And, rejoining the mid-afternoon crowds ambling in the hot spring breeze, she thought about her work colleagues who went back to their own kitchens in their own homes at the end of each day. She wondered if they, too, gave names to all their meals.

The incessant street projections begged the city workers to delay their journeys home. They showed trailers for the latest films intercut with clips of star karaoke performers, all aimed at sucking the more impressionable commuters towards the downtown Entertainment Quarter and the Repertory Domes. As the crowds neared their metro stops, high-kick dancers were scorched across the city skyline in a last-ditch attempt to prevent anyone leaving. Jayna lowered her gaze and scrutinized the footwear worn by pedestrians who rushed towards her or cut across her path. Today, she looked for shoes that demanded attention; shoes that demanded she look up to see the wearer's face. And in these faces she searched for any indication that they returned her curiosity. It didn't happen. So she stared directly into the eyes of oncoming pedestrians but she failed again; she couldn't force any connection.

She entered her residence by the side door and climbed the scrubbed stairway to her single-room quarters on the second floor, just as she had done every working day for the previous twenty-six weeks. She changed into her loose clothes and hung her suit in the narrow, open-fronted wardrobe by the sink. Dropping onto her single bed, she closed her eyes. A difficult day. She assessed her options beyond the routine of taking a shower and dining with the other residents. She could (a) chat in the common room with her friends; (b) relax alone in her room until lights out; or (c) continue her private studies. She admitted that (b) and (c) amounted to pretty much the same thing.

———

"How rare is drowning at the age of thirty-four?" Jayna said as soon as Julie seated herself at the dining table. With Julie's job at the Pensions Agency, she'd know the figures.

"Confidential…but not as rare as you might think."

Harry and Lucas briefly looked up from their meals to acknowledge Julie's remark. These four were the only diners. They ate one hour earlier than the rest of the residents at C7 because their working day was shorter by one hour. Jayna explained about Tom.

"If you consider all accidental deaths between ages thirty and thirty-five," Julie continued, "the figures are also far higher than anyone would guess. We've done a study. It seems people's natural instincts on risk are very poor."

"Care to disassemble?" said Harry.

"I'm talking historically…When primitive man lived on the savannah, the risk of accidental death was high but the types of risk were limited in number. Our intuition on certainty and uncertainty was formed then. Totally inadequate now. Life's too complex."

"Is that a problem?" said Lucas. He was the new boy.

"Yes and no. Obviously, if people underestimate certain risks they'll make decisions with unfortunate outcomes. But—" she paused and looked around her friends "—if everyone could grasp their true exposure to negative events there'd be…ramifications. People have to get on with life as though the risks aren't there. That's why everyone anticipates an average lifespan. I assume you all caught the latest news from National Statistics— *ninety-nine* years."

"So, in theory, your colleague lost two-thirds his due," said Lucas.

"I didn't understand the media's reaction," Jayna said. "What's so special about living to one hundred rather than ninety-nine?"

"Teasing failure from success," said Harry.

"Anyway, I don't believe they should massage the figures to achieve an extra year," said Julie. "They were even suggesting taking deaths through natural disasters out of the statistics. The facts are the facts."

"Well, I can tell you one thing," said Jayna. "I don't think any massaging would keep Tom Blenkinsop out of the statistics."

The group of friends fell quiet. Jayna took a piece of bread from the platter at the center of the table and chased the remaining traces of a thin gravy from her plate. Her companions registered her eagerness and, in turn, they too reached towards the bread.

———

With barely two hours of her evening remaining, Jayna returned to her small room and, prompted by Julie's remark about the savannah, she downloaded a wildlife program on the Serengeti. She turned to the cage on her bedside table. Hester had given her a branch of privet last week and it was now stripped almost bare. Observing her insects, as she always did in the evening, she jotted a note: *Leaves are consumed by an insect that looks like a twig. So what is the difference between a leaf falling and a stick insect dying?*

Out on the Serengeti, a lioness pounced at the flanks of a bolting zebra. Jayna had watched hundreds of similar murderous sequences over recent months and she recognized that only a few animals were immune to the carnivorous advances of others. She decided to formalize this thought by writing an essay on food chain hierarchies and biomass diversity. There were plenty of learned treatises already on the subject but she wouldn't consult them. She preferred to work it out for herself; it all came down to basic mathematics.

The lights in her room dimmed and she prepared herself for a twelve-hour sleep. As she lay in bed she looked into her little wildlife park and, in the remaining half-light, could just discern her twiggy roommates from their twiggy habitat. She knew Hester would bring another privet branch from the suburbs. With family to take care of, she had plenty to think about other than stick insects. And she might be preoccupied over Tom's death. But she simply wouldn't forget.

Drifting towards sleep, Jayna's mind stubbornly refused a final release. She retraced her thoughts and pinpointed a question that wandered, unresolved: how would the zebra's experience of fear differ from Tom's?

CHAPTER 2

Bound to be minuses as well as pluses, Jayna thought, *but I'd swap places for a day, if not a week.* The street cleaner leaned towards the wall gripping his lance. Dirty brick...lunge... clean brick. Methodically, he chased the yellow paint, which followed an imprecise, splattery arc across the rest station's front entrance.

Julie dived through the sweeping haze of droplets and stood with Jayna looking back at the rest station wall.

"What's all this?" said Julie.

"I asked him. He said someone's thrown yellow paint across the wall."

"That's obvious...I didn't hear anything."

"No. I didn't either...I wish I'd come out earlier."

"It probably happened during the night, Jayna."

"I meant, I like watching." Julie threw her a glance.

Jayna showed no inclination to leave.

"Well, I have to go," said Julie. "Talk later." She headed off.

Jayna half turned but kept her eyes on the lance. "Maybe we'll find out later. Someone..." Julie was halfway across the road.

The street cleaner had created a pristine scar across the dull hue of the weathered brickwork and pavement. Jayna hoped he knew what he was doing. Her right foot tapped. She transferred her weight to stop the tapping but thirty seconds later her left foot started to tap. Time to go.

Sensitized by the bright yellow violation, Jayna found herself assaulted by color along her familiar route to work, as if the cones of her retinas craved opposing bursts to counter the rude effect of the yellow. She saw, as though for the first time, the bullying daubs of the city highway engineers, the viridian ironwork of the Palace Hotel, the lipstick-red steps to the Palace Theatre's stage door, and the formless slithers and polygons of blue sky. Her attention shifted focus from colors to the surface imperfections across the U-shaped urban gorge (wall-pavement-gutter-road-gutter-pavement-wall), the misalignments, patched-in repairs. In her mind, she framed and reframed, stretched and cropped. She selected on the basis of color, selected on the basis of shape, selected on the basis of incongruity. Jayna mused to herself, *I could spend a lifetime observing this one street…*

———

Hester deposited a ribbon-handled, black-and-white striped, carrier bag at Jayna's array.

"Thanks, Hester. It's good of you to remember." As though someone prodded her in the back, she added, "What with Tom and all the upset." Hester ignored the remark and removed white tissue paper covering the bag's contents to reveal garden clippings, mainly privet. She lifted between finger and thumb a straggle of foliage from a climbing rose, and looked for approval.

"Perfect," said Jayna. And confidence renewed—she'd mentioned Tom without causing offence—she added, "Dave in Archives brings me greenery most weeks. He gets it from a park near the terminus. But he forgets sometimes."

"Well, what do you expect?" she said, as a throwaway.

Jayna's shoulders stiffened at the harshness embedded within the remark. "He's normally reliable, Hester. He keeps asking for more challenging work."

"No chance." Hester snorted. "There's no way he could cope with anything more. There are *enough* complaints about him already. *And*—" she turned and headed towards her own corner of the office "—it would be too much hassle."

That's curious, thought Jayna. She leaned back in her chair. Hester had made several objections to the idea of Dave's promotion when one overriding reason would have been more persuasive. And, to her recollection, Hester—despite being capable of minor kindnesses vis-à-vis the garden clippings—was the only person she'd heard complain about Dave. Jayna still couldn't grasp the concept behind Hester's managerial style: abbreviated politeness when she dealt with equals, and she seemed to count Jayna in that category, stretching to mere pleasantries with the directors. The directors themselves regarded her default snappiness as somehow...endearing. As for the junior analysts, like Mark...Jayna watched him, now. He was walking the long way around the office just so he didn't pass Hester's array. Jayna was sure of it. Yet, Dave, the only menial Hester had to deal with, seemed immune to—Jayna searched for the right word—her *angularity.*

She recalled a remark Hester made about Dave exactly seven weeks ago: "I swear I'll have him out of here one day." It had happened when Dave was organizing his latest sweepstake. "I don't know why he does these silly things. It's such a distraction." An overreaction by Hester, Jayna felt on reflection. Seemed harmless to her: a sweepstake for the Grand National. A major cultural event, after all. Hester had waved Dave away but he'd persisted and teased: "Go on, Hester. You've got a great chance. No-one's picked out the favorite, *Sticky Wicket.*"

She'd simply bitten a reply at him: "No. Go."

Even then, Dave hadn't given up. "Okay, I'll make the same offer to Jayna, here. You'll be sorry. Don't say—"

"She's not allowed," said Hester.

And he'd come back at her yet again. "Now come on, Hester. Let's not be a spoiler. You know you'll feel *all left out* when the race begins. And why shouldn't Jayna have—"

"Out. Now."

"All right, all right. I'm history." Which was his little joke, Jayna had subsequently learnt, coming as he did from Archives.

It struck Jayna that Hester could barely bring herself to construct a whole sentence when dealing with Dave. *I don't take that attitude with Hester*, she said to herself. *I don't think she's aware…* She wondered, as a corollary of sorts—she and Dave both being extremes, albeit on opposing sides of the bell curve—if *her* presence in the office sparked any debate, any dissent. *Are there barbed remarks when I leave the office mid-afternoon?* She turned to her array and pulled up Tom's files. *Anyway, it's beyond doubt. They all know my value. I guarantee we meet targets. And there's that proverb, one of Hester's conversation stoppers: the proof of the pudding is in the eating. She's good at that—abrupt endings.*

Late-morning, Eloise came over. "Olivia and Benjamin want to see you in the boardroom." Jayna had clinched a new correlation last week and the final report had been dispatched on Thursday to the Metropolitan Police. She was due a few words of praise. It seemed to Jayna that Mayhew McCline's directors congratulated their staff in a semi-formal setting as though executing some learned motivational strategy.

———

"Well, here's a turn-up for the books. Those correlations for violent crime looked pretty robust until half an hour ago, Jayna," said Olivia Westwood, Mayhew McCline's vice-chairman. Jayna had detected a link at regional level between violent crimes, limited though these instances were, and mean wind direction. Strong north-easterlies were the ones to watch out for.

"What's happened?"

"Whole family murdered out in Enclave S2."

Jayna felt her cheekbones burn. "It's a westerly today."

Olivia smiled. "I know, I know." Jayna had been reluctant to search for trends because the crime figures were so low. "I read your battery of provisos. Obviously, it's a crime of passion. Can't seem to stop those."

"I suggested a trend, with multiple caveats. It's not a predictive tool."

"Well, don't tell that to the client."

Olivia was a statistician herself, thought Jayna, so why did she talk like that?

"Look, we're still delighted with your conclusions and so are the police. They're going to match staff rotas to the weather forecast," said Olivia.

"Come on. Don't look so worried," said Benjamin. "It's good to make use of the crime stats. Have you seen the access costs? And after all the aggravation we had getting accreditation…"

Jayna's eyes were flicking between Benjamin and the image on the wall behind him, a large poster of *Jesse Recumbent*; a rare and monumental oak sculpture from the medieval age, of immense significance according to Olivia. *Jesse* lent gravitas to the boardroom, Jayna thought, even though he was lying down. She wondered what he'd make of Mayhew McCline and its world of trend forecasting and economic modeling. Jayna changed the subject. "Any news about Tom?"

"Not yet. How are his files?" said Benjamin.

"I checked this morning. There are a couple of ideas he abandoned that should be revived."

"He tended to dump things he wasn't interested in. What were they?"

"One on the wine industry: production trends across western Europe."

"That figures; he was teetotal. Can you handle them?"

"I don't want any distraction at the moment, Benjamin. I think you should recruit."

Benjamin groaned. "We've only just laid off Ingrid."

"Can you bring her back?" asked Olivia.

"Awkward," he said. He bared his teeth. "Bit of a slanging match, to put it mildly. I think there's something wrong there. She's far too…Anyway, never mind that. I'll find a freelance for now and brief the headhunters. Won't be easy, though. I'll have to offer more money."

"What? More than Tom was getting?" Olivia cast a glance at Jesse as if to say, *Look at what I have to deal with.* "Just do what you can," she said. And, clearly trying to calm herself, she turned to her star analyst. "So, what are you working on at the moment, Jayna?"

"Shifts in energy consumption patterns; looking at hydrogen. I'm aiming for an investment strategy report." Olivia's eyes widened. "There's plenty of data available, almost too much. I'm filtering current research projects reported in journals and conference proceedings and I'm also acquiring industrial briefing papers through more…tortuous avenues—" Benjamin nodded his approval, realizing the implication "—sifting through it all, looking for key variables. It's a big subject, so I'd rather not have any diversions."

"Okay. You've made good calls so far," said Olivia. "In fact, you've turned this department around—March figures, just being revised, will be the best ever."

"You didn't meet your predecessor Frank," said Benjamin. "We knew you'd be smarter than him but…well…you're something else." He smiled. "And far more personable. We weren't expecting that so much."

Jayna knew all about Frank; she'd seen his personnel file. In any case, she'd met plenty of Franks, and Fredas, at the rest station. Heavens, they didn't even have individual names. Why was Benjamin attempting a comparison? Frank's file revealed him to be diligent, if bland. "Brilliant at go-fetch analysis but not creative," according to Hester's filed assessment. Took his briefs, met deadlines, faultless attendance record. Deemed efficient.

"So far, so good, then?" Jayna said to Olivia. "But let me point out, please, I do become tired if I don't finish on time—" She shifted her gaze. "Benjamin, perhaps you could gently remind the team that my working day should be six hours. Remember, I'm on the job whether I'm here or at my residence. It's just the level of intensity that varies."

———

More personable? As she made her way to the elevator, she picked over Benjamin's remark.

> **personable** *adjective* **pleasant**, agreeable, likeable, nice, amiable, affable, charming, congenial, genial, engaging, pleasing; attractive, presentable, good-looking, nice-looking, pretty, appealing; *Scottish* couthy; *Scottish & N. English* bonny, canny; *dated* taking.

Before she could reach any conclusion, she needed to answer one specific question: did her appearance have any bearing on how she was regarded?

There was no full-length mirror at Mayhew McCline, or at the rest station for that matter, but when she boarded the elevator she saw a fuzzy version of herself reflected in the matte metallic doors; no detail, just an impression. She stood alongside two other female employees, benchmarks. She puckered her lips and made an assessment. Average. Neither tall nor short, neither curvaceous nor thin. An interesting negative shape between her mid-brown hair and shoulders. None of her colleagues' idiosyncratic features: high forehead, short nose, heavy jaw, receding chin, small eyes, thick eyebrows, narrow shoulders, legs disproportionate to torso, small head.

Her only feature transgressing the average was the fractionally wider setting of her eyes. Otherwise…nothing.

No, the way I look must have a neutral impact.

Jayna stepped out of the elevator and walked directly to the washroom. In the cubicle, once again, she stood facing the cold tiles. *Talent, Pure and Simple.* Quite a slogan. And it was true. She could handle colossal amounts of data, vastly more than bionics like Hester, Benjamin, and the rest of them. They had cognitive implants just as she did, but their enhancements were built on a fundamentally impoverished base. They didn't realize, Jayna thought, simply could not grasp…

The washroom door opened and someone stepped into the neighboring cubicle. Jayna sat down and urinated. She needed more time to think. No doubt, Olivia and Benjamin had pored over the details before they'd committed to her lease, even if they didn't fully appreciate the implications.

Simulant Operative Version CS12.01.

Maker: Constructor Holdings plc.

Product Description: Biological simulant, grown in vitro *from a genetic master-type characterized by prodigious analytical attributes. Widespread additional genetic interventions. Extensive bionic cognitive implants. Initiated, at Constructor Holdings' Initiation Centre in Oxford, with multi-lifetime experiential data for higher socio-economic groupings.*

The next bit translated into *more personable* but they probably missed the point:

Wider range of emotional capabilities than earlier versions (the Franks and Fredas) *to refine social behavior, leading to enhanced assimilation within the workforce and exceptional skills in continuous learning.*

To herself, Jayna said, *That word* assimilation, *it's the wrong one to use. It's an engineer's word. I'm far better than Frank because I fit in; I'm one of the team, the best member of the team.* Embedded Intelligence, *another slogan. That's a fair description, too. I can discuss, advise, mentor. Apart from the odd faux pas, they think I'm the best thing...since sliced bread. Yes, I fit in, I'm more personable. But, to pin it down, I can empathize:*

> **empathize,** *verb*: **identify**, sympathize, be in sympathy, understand, share someone's feelings, be in tune; be on the same wavelength as; relate to, feel for, have insight into; *informal* put oneself in someone else's shoes.

———

Hester returned from a long lunch with her stockbroker buddies, halted mid-office alongside Jayna's array and announced, marginally more chilled than her usual self: "Okay, I'd better warn you all, I'm bringing Jon-Jo to work tomorrow morning. Three hours max. Definitely not office trained."

"I'd love to meet him, Hester. Why is he—?"

Hester cut her off. "Having his pre-3s check late morning," she said, addressing everyone. "Daniel's stuck in a meeting for a couple of hours, and when that's finished we'll go together to the hospital."

Jayna had no experience of children beyond witnessing their antics in the Entertainment Quarter. Even there, she and her friends stayed away from kids' events. This could be her only opportunity, possibly for months to come, to speak one-to-one with a young person. So, during the afternoon, she scanned the statistics on child-related markets and, on the basis of this snap analysis, she left work as normal at three-thirty and headed straight for the Talking Horse Toy Shop located down a back lane off Peter Street.

———

None of the business premises had street numbers but from the end of the still-cobbled lane Jayna caught the shining eyes of stuffed creatures. As she approached she distinguished a teddy bear in dungarees, a rag-hatted doll, five squashy elephants trunk-to-tail across the window front, a tearful clown (why, thought Jayna, would anyone buy *that* for a child?), and a painted green dragon suspended in a tortured pose by puppeteer's cords. A bell clattered overhead as she entered. Would she find anything for Jon-Jo, she wondered, that cost less than a week's allowance? On a round table, small toys were piled into baskets with a hand-painted label stuck between them stating *Party Bag Gifts*. Jayna read and re-read the phrase and wondered if a hyphen were missing. She explored the surfaces of these modest offerings until her fingertips met polished wood—a giraffe standing on a cylindrical base. She held it up and saw that each of its legs, and its neck, comprised a series of cylindrical forms.

"Push the base up," said the shop assistant. Jayna turned and inclined her head.

"Go on. Push the base up with your thumb."

She did so and the giraffe collapsed, its head hanging below the base. Startled, she withdrew her thumb, and the giraffe leapt to its full height, elegant and poised, ready to chew from lush canopies once again.

"The simplest toys are usually the best," he said.

"Do you gift wrap?"

"Well, I suppose so. It won't take much wrapping." He laughed. "Did you never have one of these as a child?"

She hesitated. "No. I didn't."

He wrapped. She turned away. The muscles tensed around her mouth. She paid with the exact coinage and left, the eyes of a polar bear following her down the lane as she considered the implications of the shopkeeper's seemingly innocuous inquiry.

A childhood. Why did he ask such a personal question?

Looking down at the shining package she noticed the assistant had tucked a Talking Horse calling card under the ribbon ties. She grabbed the card, pushed the package under her arm, and ripped the card once, twice, and three times into eight horribly irregular pieces. She crumpled the fragments between her fingers. But her actions were too puny. With an exaggerated arm movement, as though lifting a brick, she threw the paper scraps to the ground and stamped on them, scuffing them into the pavement. Jayna steadied herself, her hand against brickwork, and turned to look up and then down the lane. No one. She leaned against the wall, her right arm still registering aftershocks from the exertion.

So impertinent. Her heart raced.

She counted to calm herself. But other thoughts insisted: her colleagues…going home to their housemates, or their children. Such long lives—twenty, thirty, forty-plus years—from babies. So slow, so incremental. No perceptible change between one day and the next. "Oh! Look how she's grown." She recalled the cooing chorus when Benjamin showed projections of eight-year-old Alice. It seemed to be a cause of genuine incredulity. And then, she remembered it clearly, a dissection of the child's appearance: her father's eyes, her mother's hair. And Benjamin: "Yes, she's certainly got the best of us both."

And I expect she played with a toy wooden giraffe…

———

By the time C7 came in sight, her breathing had steadied but her arm still ached. She scrutinized the rest station from across the street.

A ghosting of the splattered paint was detectable across the brickwork. Maybe the paint had been shot at the wall accidentally, somehow. It didn't make any sense, just throwing paint. But, then, Tom's
drowning didn't make sense. Neither did a lot of things, she thought.

———

As ever, the dinner served in C7 was untitled. Some sort of meat sub-
stitute, vegetables, potatoes; the usual plain offerings. But, the canteen
assistant poured a sauce with a jarring citrus aroma. Jayna leaned
towards the serving hatch. "What's the name of this evening's meal?"

The canteen assistant dropped his ladle. "Doesn't 'av' a name,"
he said. "We were just told to make a fruit sauce."

"It's unexpected. Thank you," Jayna said, and smiled.

This seemed to disarm him and, apparently unsure of himself, he
added, "Well, if it were on a piece of duck yer'd call it Duck Aloringe."

"I'm sure everyone will like it."

"Yer not all gettin' it. Just you lot on first sittin'."

Joining Harry and Julie, she said, "There's no orange sauce for
the Franks and Fredas."

"Well, it must be a directive of some sort," said Harry.

Lucas dived towards the table, bundled himself into his chair;
his knees collided with the table leg—everyone winced—and his
dinner plate and glass of water slid sideways on his tray. Ignoring
the spilt water, he spread his hands flat either side of the tray. "Something *weird*—" he stalled, as though realizing he'd never needed this
word before "—came through our department today. Should have
been encrypted for the chief executive's office. It wasn't, though no
one paid any attention—"

"What are you trying to say, Lucas? Get to the point," said
Harry, not unkindly.

"It *said*—" he paused "—that my counterpart in the Merseyside
Tax Office has been sent back to the Constructor. He was spotted

dining in an Indian restaurant two weeks ago having—" he checked his friends' expressions "—a *Lamb Biryani*. It seems he'd saved his weekly allowance over several months, contravened his directive to eat only at the Civil Service and rest station canteens."

"Why would he do that?" said Julie, a piece of Duck Aloringe on her raised fork. "What was the point?"

"I don't know. I didn't know what to make of it." And evidently eager to remain the center of attention, he added, "I didn't hear anything else on the subject. But, I can tell you…I was surprised."

For several minutes they ate their meals in silence. Julie finished her last mouthful and said, "About the yellow paint…It also happened at C5 last night."

"How do you know?" said Jayna.

"I was in a meeting today with someone from C5. She mentioned it." Julie was in no hurry to elaborate but after several seconds she said, "It seems they didn't finish the job on our wall. At their rest station, the word *No* was scraped through the paint, with an exclamation mark added for good measure."

"They must have been disturbed," said Harry.

"Mentally unstable?" said Lucas.

"No, Lucas, they were *interrupted*," said Harry.

"But…it's a silly way of sending a message. And what were they saying *No* to?"

"Isn't that obvious, Lucas? They must be saying *No* to us," said Julie, calmly.

"It's a bit late for that," said Harry.

"But who did it?" asked Lucas.

"What does it matter?" said Harry.

It occurred to Jayna that both Julie and Harry worked in the government sector. As did Lucas. Jayna let this thought roam for a few moments. Maybe it lay in the process-heavy nature of their jobs; it dampened their inquisitiveness. Maybe Lucas would drift the same way.

CHAPTER 3

At **09:37 hours, Hester and her boy** came blustering into the office. One wing of Hester's shirt collar lay flat, the other pointed skywards. She groaned under the weight of three soft but bulging multi-colored bags. A strap slipped off her shoulder and Hester simply dragged the bag along the carpet. Jayna sat transfixed. The bags alone offered her a glimpse into Hester's life away from the office. These were her private things, chosen for a family purpose. In the starchy surroundings of Mayhew McCline they looked out of place.

"Here comes trouble," called Benjamin. Indulgent smiles rippled across the analysts' floor. The appearance of one small child had instantaneously changed the mood of the office as if the spell cast by Tom's death had been broken.

Maybe, Jayna wondered, they needed an excuse to change mode.

Hester streamed her apology: "Sorry, everyone, but Jon-Jo isn't a morning person. It was murder trying to get him ready. And, my God, commuting with a two-year-old is *hell*. Nearly trampled underfoot." Turning to Jon-Jo, she lowered her voice and raised her pitch: "Okay, Jon-Jo. Now, let's get you settled in next to me. Here's your bag of toys and your blanket. Why don't you have a play while I do my work and then I'll give you a little snack?"

He moaned and dropped to the floor. "Thirsty now, Mummy."

"Right. Okay, then." She riffled through a second bag. "Here, some nibbles and your drink. Be careful with it, all right?" She looked around the room seemingly vexed that she, for once, was the source of disturbance. But for Jayna, Jon-Jo's appearance was a welcome development. This was the real thing: *primary research*.

And so, Hester fired up her array while Jon-Jo sat on the floor and grazed through his snack, dropping crumbs down his clothes and tossing his drink aside. He rolled onto his stomach and played with his toy figures, smashing two of them together in his little fists. This rough treatment went on for some time but then he calmed down and lay flat, only he repeatedly lifted his right foot and brought it back down, just catching a waste bin which clanged against the side of his mother's work array. Jayna studied him closely. Surely the boy knew this noise was anti-social.

Eventually Hester looked down at her son. "Come on, Jon-Jo. Please stop kicking the bin. Stand next to me and do some drawing." He struggled to his feet and took the stubby marker, drawing big circles, round and round and round, the sheet refusing to stay still under his enthusiasm. He shook the marker to create a new color and stabbed at the paper, three stabs to the second.

"What are you drawing, Jon-Jo?" called Jayna.

"It's rainin'!" he shouted. Stab, stab, stab. He pushed the picture to the floor and started on another.

"Drawing is a very physical activity for Jon-Jo," said Eloise as she walked through the office.

"Doesn't *do* minimal," said Hester.

Jayna continued to observe. Having run out of sheets, Jon-Jo glanced sideways at his mother and surreptitiously began coloring his fingernails, shaking the marker so that each nail had its own color. He lay down again and made small but vivid marks on the floor. Perhaps he thought no one would notice. More likely, he was making a point in his own childish way, Jayna thought. These marks might be a needling reminder to his mother: don't forget me, Jon-Jo. Almost territorial.

The boy continued for a further hour and a half, constantly pushing at the boundaries of acceptable behavior. Twice, Hester led him to the washroom and each time he stamped his feet across the office while shouting: "I'm marchin'. I'm a soldier."

At lunchtime the boy's father, Daniel, appeared. "How's he been?"

"Pretty good, actually," said Hester, breezily. She walked with Jon-Jo and Daniel out to the elevators. The wide-eyed soldier once again stamped his feet.

Jayna intercepted their path. "Hester, may I give this to Jon-Jo?"

"Yes. Of course."

So Jayna crouched down and handed the neatly wrapped present to the boy. "Here you are, Jon-Jo. Something to play with when you get back to your home." He seemed mesmerized by the shining surfaces and showed no inclination to prise open the wrapping.

"How sweet of you, Jayna," said Hester. She stooped down to the boy and whispered conspiratorially, "Say thank-you, Jon-Jo." Which he did.

Everyone called out: "Bye, Jon-Jo, bye, Daniel."

The tousled ambience of the office gradually settled closer to its usual steady-state until the junior analyst Rebecca pouted and in a fake tantrum shouted, "I want a coffee. Now!" And the sound of slow laughter extended the newly softened vibe at Mayhew McCline.

Curious, thought Jayna.

And as if the lightened atmosphere had allowed freethinking and unforced connections to occur, she arrived at a new conclusion on a lesser, more speculative, vein of research. For Jayna had been exploring, over recent days, the language embodied in the Letters to Shareholders signed by the bosses of two hundred listed companies in their latest Annual Reports. She had checked the syntax, the occurrence of collocation and metonymies, and the usage of euphemism, idiom, and metaphor. Off went a summary to Benjamin:

> **Project Ref J132**—*An Examination of Letters to Shareholders and Correlations with Performance.*
>
> **Resource**—*The most recent Annual Reports for two hundred companies listed on the London Stock Exchange, and Quarterly Figures reported subsequently.*
>
> **Analysis**—*Linguistic.*
>
> **Summary**—*Regardless of company turnover, there is a strong correlation between the use of nautical metaphor in a company's Letter to Shareholders and a subsequent downturn in quarterly results.*
>
> **Comment**—*This correlation, in my opinion, reflects the fact that many nautical metaphors refer to difficult weather conditions. Other common metaphors—those relating to cricket, for example—have more positive connotations. The choice of nautical metaphor might be unwitting but may well reveal a high level of pessimism among the board of directors that they are reluctant to acknowledge openly.*

A quick response: *Hoist the main sail. We'll make headway with that one. B.*

———

The New Cantonese Restaurant and Buffet beckoned Jayna on her return to Granby Row. Located in a basement on Whitworth Street, the buffet tempted passers-by with an array of steaming, unnaturally colorful dishes; Jayna glanced down and tried to guess their names. She hoped to identify Singapore Style Rice Vermicelli, a name that Jayna found herself mouthing as soon as she saw the restaurant. But today, Jayna decided it would be foolish to linger. She didn't even

break her stride and the slight turn of her head was sufficiently lazy
to conceal the true depth of her interest.

———

"Real sausages," Harry announced as Jayna took her seat in the canteen, "and nicely creamed potatoes."

"I can't smell much difference," said Julie. "But they do taste
better than the other sausages. It's more complex."

Jayna tapped her foot. She wished she had Hester's ability to
guillotine a conversation. "We had a small visitor to the office today," she said, abruptly. They looked confused. "Small, not short,"
she said. "A child, just two years old."

"Ah, ha!" said Harry. They all smiled.

"It was so confusing. His behavior was erratic. I can't work out
if he *knew* he was naughty. And, if he *didn't* know, how will he im-
prove his behavior as he gets older?"

Lucas and Julie looked upwards as though the answer hovered
above Jayna's head. They looked back at Jayna with the blankness
of people caught mid-daydream. She realized they were picking,
unsuccessfully, at the interstices between the knowledge they gained
at initiation and their real-world encounters. Neither Lucas at
the Tax Office nor Julie at the Pensions Agency were primed on
anthropology—fit for purpose—but Jayna hoped Harry, with his
experience at the Society Department, would cast some light.

With no one else offering any explanation, he weighed in,
as Jayna had anticipated, in expert mode. "Young people—"
he put his knife and fork down and pushed back his shoulders
"—relinquish their anti-social childhood behavior patterns if they
follow a normal line of development. Positive reinforcement for
good behavior and so on. And then brain implants at the age of
eighteen make them far more rational." End of subject, as far as
Harry was concerned.

"So, initially, it all depends on monitoring by parents and teachers," said Jayna.

"That's an interesting point. Parents would like you to think otherwise but we've had a review at the department concluding that teachers play a much more important role..." He threw his hands out. "They have more time. They focus on behavioral issues and developing wider curiosities in the children so that, in later life, they can pursue special interests in their leisure time."

"That's true," said Jayna. "My boss, Olivia, is an amateur authority on medievalism. She keeps replicas of historical artifacts in her office and then there's *Jesse Recumbent*."

Harry wasn't listening. "Implantation, you see, frees up teachers' time. They just cover the basics for children who will remain fully organic. If they're never implanted they can at least read and write properly. No point bothering with more."

The canteen assistant lumbered past their table, glanced at Jayna, and said, "Bangers 'n' Mash."

———

Back in her room, Jayna pulled the rest station handbook from the top of her wardrobe and tore out a page. She made a series of creases and folds to form a long slim sleeve. She slid the tiny corpse of the second-smallest stick insect into the paper shroud and laid it in her palm. After a moment's contemplation, she placed the shroud atop the handbook and lifted them both onto the wardrobe. Safe there, for now. And with the corpse dealt with, she set about cleaning the cage, collecting the droppings and tiny eggs that lay intermingled on the cage floor. One day, she would raise some nymphs. They would all be female, which was a shame; she'd like the extra variable.

Carausius morosus, Indian walking stick. Wingless. Up to ten centimeters in length. Lifespan: one year. Parthenogenetic

*reproduction: only one in ten thousand nymphs is male. Incomplete
metamorphosis: egg, nymph, adult. Nymphs moult five or six times
by shedding their exoskeleton.*

———

Cleaning job finished, Jayna lay curled up on her bed and allowed
her thoughts to be dictated by whatever fell under her gaze. The
joints between the architrave and the skirting board always screamed
at her when she lay facing the door. The skirting board had been cut
three centimeters too short and a small piece of wood had been
pushed in to fill the gap. But no amount of paint could ever conceal
the poor workmanship. No doubt, the joiner had failed to appreciate how many minutes and hours of irritation this error would
cause over subsequent years.

And then, the dressing gown hanging from a single hook on the
back of the plain-faced door. Jayna became aware she was describ-
ing how the garment hung as a set of equations—approximated,
for she wasn't trying too hard—equations that described the peaks
and troughs of all the folds. She allowed the dinner conversation
to seep into her thoughts. *Do bionics like Hester and Benjamin play
with mathematics in the same way? If I were an organic, even a smart
organic like Dave, would I see a hanging garment and think about the
folds or would I simply…see it?*

As she climbed into the warm bed a cold thought crept in
beside her. *The joiner's mistakes are no worse than my own.* The lights
started to fade. *A westerly wind, one dead family. The smallest stick
insect, still thriving.* The room was dark and all she could see was a
line of light tracing the door. *And, now, there's no Tom. Didn't expect
that. Not even on my radar.*

CHAPTER 4

Craig and Dave stood toe-to-toe in front of the elevators and passed notes and coins back and forth, clearly making a deal of some precision. But, then, Craig would not approximate even over a jar of home-made honey. Jayna knew this was the core of their transaction. She approached them along the spinal corridor of Mayhew McCline. It seemed incongruous—Craig handling coinage—because day in, day out he dealt with columns of numbers relating to sums of money exchanged in the digital ether. Here was the head of Accounts buying honey from the junior archivist, a sideline officially condoned by Olivia. But Jayna recalled an outburst by Hester: "I never eat any of it. I pour it down the sink as soon as I get home. I mean, *where have those bees been?*"

Craig peeled off and Jayna raised her eyebrows at Dave. "How's business?"

"Pretty lively." They waited together for the elevator. After a few moments, he turned to her. "Do you ever get bored, Jayna?"

"No, Dave. I don't suppose I do." And trying to sound bright, "You always seem busy."

"Well, I'm inventive. I'm bored out of my fucking head, really." Her back felt clammy.

frustrate: *verb.* 1. prevent (a plan or action) from progressing, succeeding, or being fulfilled; prevent (someone) from doing or achieving something; 2. cause (someone) to feel dissatisfied or unfulfilled. *Adj.* archaic frustrated.

An image flashed across her mind: scraps of paper on a pavement with a fragment of the Talking Horse Toy Shop logo. She wanted to ease the tension. "Let's talk sometime, Dave. I'd like to know what you do outside of work. You know, your hobbies."

"Yeah. Well, maybe. Come up and see my bees sometime." Dave rubbed the back of his head with his right hand. "You're not like the other analysts, are you? So up their own arses." He looked over his shoulder to check that no one had overheard. As if embarrassed by his own remark, he changed the subject. "Your stick insects all right?"

"A bit sluggish."

He laughed. "Jayna, you cracked a joke." The elevator doors opened and they stepped in. Dave punched the button.

"Well, it wouldn't work with Latin names," she said.

"That's true." He leaned against the side wall of the elevator. "S'pose you've heard the rumor about Tom Blenkinsop?"

"What rumor?"

"There was a note."

"A note? What do you mean?"

"A suicide note." *Ping*! The elevator doors opened. "You haven't heard?" They stepped out and lingered awkwardly.

"How do you know?" she said.

"Someone overheard. It's doing the rounds now." They both detected Olivia's voice, approaching.

"Got to go," said Jayna. She set off down the glass-walled corridor, spurning the squared floor pattern, which would normally have dictated her stride length. Benjamin walked across his office to greet her. He guided her to his meeting area by placing his hand in the small of her back and applying a slight pressure.

"Take a seat, Jayna. I want this preliminary because you've not had an appraisal before. Just want to make sure you know the format."

She sat on the sofa and covered her face with her hands.

"What's the matter? What did I miss?"

"I have to tell you, Benjamin. I should have told you before."

"Told me what?"

She looked up. "Tom sent me a report to finish...I told him I was too busy to help. He was very upset, really angry with me. And then, he went on holiday upset, and committed suicide. I think it's my fault."

"Suicide?" shouted Benjamin.

"Everyone knows about the note."

"A note? There's no suicide note. His brother would have told me. Though...Ha! Funny, ha! He did leave a note...for *me*, tendering his bloody resignation. Poached by Stanthorpe's for a fifty per cent hike in salary. That's why he booked a last-minute holiday—he was using up all his entitlement."

"Oh."

"Jesus, Jayna! How did you jump to that conclusion, that *you* pushed him into...*suicide?*"

"Well, it seemed too much of a coincidence."

"But it would be completely disproportionate. Can't you see that?" said Benjamin.

"I suppose...Sorry, Benjamin, I got the wrong—"

"Okay. Let's order some tea, calm down and start again." And as an afterthought, "I'll have to stop that bloody rumor now."

After some twenty minutes' mock appraisal, Benjamin cut the air with outspread hands. "Enough. Let's go off record. How are other things going? Working hours and so on."

"Fine."

"Because I noticed you were here early today. If you're working too hard then you will jump to irrational conclusions."

It was true. She had turned up before the other analysts to steam through some personal research. She'd downloaded research papers on child development, *The General Practitioner*'s articles on food cravings (was Lamb Biryani a common craving?), University of Warwick research into the olfactory senses, together with 1,143 linked resources, which oddly led her to historical crime stats organized according to perpetrator status and crime category.

"I wanted to spend more time preparing for this meeting. And, to compensate, I plan to leave the office earlier this afternoon." Had he looked through her downloads? She should offer more. As she stood to leave the meeting, she added, "By the way, I'm doing some wildcat research at present. I'm taking a broader look at crime stats. It isn't a high priority but I'll let you know if anything interesting emerges."

"You said you were busy with the energy stuff. You didn't want distractions."

"It's back-burner research, Benjamin, rather like the Letters to Shareholders. Research without any guaranteed commercial outcome. That's why I'm allocating a very low priority. But I have a hunch…And I still hold the classified crime data. We must make full use before our access approval comes up for renewal."

"Okay. But don't get carried away. Let me know before you increase its status. You're the one concerned about your working hours."

"Fine."

"Anything else you want to raise?"

She seized the opportunity. "There *is*, as a matter of fact. I've been wondering…I think it would be an excellent idea for me to see a few home environments. I was fascinated by Jon-Jo yesterday…I know I'd need authorization and I'd need invitations…"

"I'm not sure. Leave it with me." Benjamin guided her towards his door by placing his hand behind her arm. His hand slid towards her elbow.

She stopped in her tracks and turned towards her boss. "Jayna, I'm sorry. Really. It's in the small print, I know."

———

An internal communication flagged *Sad News* hit everyone's array shortly after lunchtime:

> *I'm sorry, yet relieved, to inform you all that Tom Blenkinsop's body has been found by the local coastguard. An autopsy is required before the body can be released to the family. However, when funeral arrangements are eventually finalized, Mayhew McCline staff will be informed and anyone wishing to attend will be given time off to do so. If any of you are struggling with this sudden loss and require counseling, please contact HR.*
>
> *Olivia*

Why would counseling help, wondered Jayna? Why would talking about Tom's death to a professional be any different to chatting with colleagues? Scheduling a meeting with HR seemed so unnecessary. The junior analysts, she noticed, were congregating yet again in the kitchen. *And, after all, it's not as though anyone here were related to him.*

———

Leaving precisely twenty minutes early, Jayna called into the small floristry tucked into the ground floor retail outlets below Mayhew McCline. Some succulent foliage might prevent any further malaise among her stick insects. The second smallest, she thought, had never had a name…Eloise kept a projection of her cat at work; it wandered around her work array. She called it Freud but Jayna could make no connection. So puzzling. People seemed to harbor a delusion that animals were like them, thought like them, which, of course, they patently could not, any more than the pigeons in the park or her stick insects. Why didn't they just appreciate animals, birds, insects for that matter, for what they were? *Obviously, I have my own proper name. I am perfectly human, as organic as any bionic. Much smarter of—*

"Yes, love? Is that all you want, just that bit of greenery?"

Jayna held out a limp straggle of variegated ivy. "Yes, it's for my stick insects." She presented a particularly endearing smile.

"Take some of these offcuts instead. I won't charge you. My nephew has stick insects and he says they really gobble up rose leaves, and they like all types of ivy. It's all organic, too. No pesticides. You see, I know about stick insects. My nephew tells me everything."

"Thank you, that's really very helpful. It's difficult to find the right kind of greenery in the city center. I depend on handouts from friends." A look of pained resignation crossed Jayna's face.

"Well, call in any time. It's only going to waste. And if Geena's here instead of me, tell her it's all right with Prudence."

"Thanks, Prudence."

The assistant wrapped the offcuts as if dealing with a Valentine's gift. Jayna took hold of the precious package and murmured, "My name's Jayna."

The tentative nature of her statement provoked a gently spoken response: "That's a nice name." Prudence evidently recognized a less robust creature than herself.

On her way out, Jayna nodded to her reflection in a mirror behind the flower racks.

She set off for C7, merging with a mish-mash of adults who walked with greater or lesser determination in the direction of the Library Theatre. She walked in step with the two people nearest to her. *Walk the same streets, breathe the same air.* And she considered carefully the range of people she'd met over the past six months—her colleagues, her friends, the staff at C7, and now Prudence. *I inhabit their worlds and they inhabit mine; it's a seductive thought. But…do some people inhabit other people's lives in a more...demonstrative, more invasive manner? Maybe I should see it differently.* She conjured a three-dimensional timeline with thousands of colored tubes weaving in and out. *Our lives run parallel for a while then intersect or shoot off. Take Jon-Jo—he'll have more intersections than I ever will.*

A young man ran past Jayna from behind, the flapping material of his jacket making violent contact with hers. In that instant, she saw zebras bolting...and a lioness...teeth and claws sinking into striped flanks. A bloodied mouth.

———

She was the first resident to return to the rest station that afternoon. A lengthy, uninterrupted dousing in the communal shower offered a cure for how she felt, which was...unsettled: an unsatisfactory negative. In truth, she longed to feel waves crashing over her, just like the images she'd seen above the Opera House last week, an advertisement for surfing holidays in Cornwall.

The bathroom was deserted. She undressed, adjusted the shower controls for maximum pressure, and allowed the water jets to blast and abrade her skin. Within a minute, her skin became reddened and sore. She turned slowly, and repeatedly, through 360 degrees so that water was constantly flowing down her unmarked skin. After two minutes, there was no appreciable temperature difference between the front and back of her torso. She became hot and then hotter still. What would happen, she wondered, if she didn't stop? Like a child twizzing around, and around, and around, just for the experience, not caring for the consequences. She increased the water temperature. After a further three minutes, the room was filled with dense white steam and she felt light and lost. The whiteness absorbed her. And, as she continued turning, perspiration evacuated her skin, flowing in sheets. She felt a dull ache throughout her body. At last, she stilled herself, allowing the jets to shoot needles at her flat belly, her small breasts. As blackness closed in, she felt repeated spasms deep inside and her body buckled.

She regained consciousness. It might have been five seconds or five minutes. Staggering around the shower room, her right shoulder and knee throbbing, she pushed open a window and turned off the hot jets. Then, lurching towards the toilet cubicles, she retched and for the first time in her life she saw the semi-digested remains of her previous meal.

———

Jayna lay aching and unmoving on her bed. *What's wrong with me? I acted like a child and I nearly killed myself.* Remembering the final moments before she collapsed, she saw the white steam clouds and the black halo, which first filled the edges of her vision and then closed down her senses completely. She rewound, and recalled the pounding hot jets and the deep spasms. They seemed to come from nowhere as though a button had been pressed.

Her bedside companions twitched. She mustered a groan.

Her head was in a vice and she felt bruised. But she knew she ought to eat something. If she didn't appear in the canteen she'd have to offer some explanation tomorrow. Or, worse still, her friends would call by her room later.

———

Approaching the serving hatches a new, slightly-too-sweet aroma hit her, just what she didn't need. The canteen assistant looked up in her direction and proffered his slowly enunciated, open vowels: "Somethin' special today. Lemon chicken with spicy noodles." Confirmed by a new text display.

"Is this a menu?"

"Sort of. It's what we've got to do now. Orders from above. We 'ad some big toffs down 'ere askin' all sorts of daft questions."

"Oh? What about?"

"What food got wasted. If you residents liked some meals better than others. Things like that."

"Well we don't comment on the food, usually."

"That's what I said. But then they wanted to know if any of you lot had said anything at all, y'know, out of the ordinary." Their eyes fixed, for a moment only. He turned away. "I told them: 'What yer on about? 'Course no one's said owt.'"

"Right," said Jayna. And she took her tray, feeling the weight pulling through her right arm on her bruised shoulder. Why didn't he tell them? And why was he letting her know he didn't tell them? By the time she reached her table she'd decided the explanation was simple. He didn't like the toffs with the daft questions. He felt no obligation to cooperate. And he must be trying to warn her. *Warn?*

"How's the food?" she said to her companions, hoping to distract attention away from her inflamed face and neck. She was still steaming hot.

Julie looked up and Jayna was taken aback to see her looking… forlorn? "There's been another recall, Jayna. Another of our generation."

"Not around here," said Lucas, jumping in.

"Another?" said Jayna. And with studied calm, "But why?"

"All I know," said Lucas, "is that a female was taken out of service as a result of erratic time-keeping at work."

"Which was where?" said Jayna.

"The Institute of Forensic Accountancy near Birmingham. They have links with the Tax Office and I had dealings with them over a particularly complex case of evasion, which—"

"But, Lucas, what was the cause of her poor time-keeping?" said Jayna.

"I don't know. I was simply informed that Nicole had left. My colleagues gleaned a little more information and I overheard them." Jayna could imagine Lucas straining to listen in, just so he could report back. "Apparently, she'd missed a critical meeting and had also been absent without specific reason on a number of other occasions."

"And that merited a recall?" said Harry.

"They can't afford to take any risk with a breakthrough model," said Jayna. "The research and development costs have been astronomical so they'll want to maintain customer confidence. I suppose the Constructor could instigate a general recall but that would damage the brand severely, impact the subsequent uptake of new leases." The sounds of knives and forks contacting crockery seemed to amplify as Jayna waited for some response.

Julie raised the question on Jayna's mind. "Why should this start now? This never happened with the Franks, as far as we know."

"I think a general recall will be unavoidable if this carries on," said Jayna.

"But maybe it won't make much difference anyway," said Harry. "If the Constructor saves our extended knowledge, we could be re-initiated and sent back to work."

"If there were a complete recall, it would be a crisis measure aimed at rescuing some market credibility," said Jayna. The others nodded. She had deftly disguised her own uncertainty. However, she imagined she'd be quite a different person after reinitiation.

"There's something else," said Harry, reluctantly. "More yellow paint, at C3 and C8."

———

Having changed into her pajamas, newly laundered, Jayna performed her bedtime rituals. At her small sink, she washed her face, cleaned her teeth, applied face cream, and brushed her hair, all with standard issue kit, all on automatic. The Nicole incident in Birmingham was eating at her and, while her thoughts ricocheted, her background processing on the latest regional crime statistics flagged up a data snippet within the restricted files. *I could leave it for now. It can easily wait till tomorrow…Maybe unwise; that westerly wind…I need to tighten up.*

And so, she focused on a spike in public affray incidents. Jayna held the sides of the sink with both hands and leaned forward as she considered the implications. She knew the authorities ignored a significant level of riot within the organic community out in the enclaves. But the latest figures included five GBH cases committed by organics on their bionic superiors. No such cases in the past nine months. With the back of her hand she brushed a stray hair from the basin edge. She'd seen no media reports; suppressed? If she could clarify the situation, find any indicators…She smacked her hand hard against the basin. She should have detected something awry before now. There was always a telltale within the historical data and she'd been trawling for months. It must be there. Why hadn't she seen anything?

The room was now in darkness and she banged her sore knee as she fumbled her way into bed. Lying on her side, she stroked the fresh sheets with the inside of her foot. This small act always soothed her but tonight the ritual's potency failed.

When eventually she did fall into sleep, the day's events crowded her dreams in bizarre juxtapositions. Benjamin and Hester were dining with her in the rest station discussing their tax returns, Hester arguing she shouldn't have to pay a brass farthing. She kept repeating, "Not a single brass farthing." Tom carried a tray loaded with mugs of steaming tea and tried desperately to persuade everyone they weren't poisoned. He was pathetic: "I made them myself." Then, her stick insects gave birth, somehow, to male nymphs and she fed them honey. Most bizarre of all, Jayna soaped herself in the communal shower with Dave from Archives. At which point, daybreak was announced, not by birdsong but by the clumsy removal of recycling units from below her second floor window.

Her dreamworld sloughed away and a name, wrapped around an invisible ball—it bounced, bounced, bounced through her mind. Taniyama…Yutaka Taniyama. She stretched and smiled. Yes, he made plenty of mistakes.

CHAPTER 5

Jayna **squinted against the piercing sunlight** as she emerged from the side entrance of C7. Turning right, and then left, would take her along the shortest route to Mayhew McCline. She stepped down to the pavement and stopped. She looked up and down the street. What would Taniyama do? Tilting her face to the sky, she summoned back the words she'd recalled while stirring from sleep that morning: *He was gifted with the special capability of making many mistakes, mostly in the right direction.* The soles of her feet tingled. Yutaka Taniyama's collaborator Goro Shimura had written these words of high praise thirty years after Taniyama's suicide, in an article, "Very Personal Recollections," published in the *Bulletin of the London Mathematical Society.*

Poor Shimura, thought Jayna. No matter how hard he'd tried, he had failed to emulate his friend's intuitive daring. Shimura admitted he was, by nature, simply too methodical.

The Taniyama–Shimura Conjecture: a mid-twentieth century discovery—too fantastical to be taken seriously at first—that modular forms and elliptic curves were one and the same thing. This conjecture opened the possibility that all mathematical realms are related. When Andrew Wiles extended their conjecture he was able to prove Pierre de Fermat's Last Theorem and in doing so made

headline news around the world. Here was a theorem that math-
ematicians had failed to prove for 358 years and yet it underpinned
many areas of number theory.

She turned left and left again, heading north. She strode, long
and languid, across the veldt. *There's nothing wrong with making*
mistakes—Taniyama proved the point—as long as one's intuition is
sound. That's where I fall down. That's my problem. My world is too
small. My experiences…too few, too repetitive. I must search out the
extremities, meet the unexpected…feel the true texture of life. And as
she negotiated her less-than-direct route to work, she formulated
the basis of her plan:

An Experiment: To introduce random activity into daily routines,
forcing a shift into uncharted territory and new experiences.

Her actions in the shower were a perfect example. She had to
take risks, just as Jon-Jo would. Don't think of the consequences,
she instructed herself. Act!

Jayna already felt disorientated. A new road, fewer vehicles,
more pedestrians, different sounds, a side street lined with
cherry trees. She touched the pole of a metro stop, just a red dot
on a map before today. And new faces. If she took a different
route each day, would she eventually register all the people who
worked in this commercial district? She cast her thoughts to
demographics: the size of the working population, modes of
transport, working hours. A 90 per cent probability of encoun-
tering 35 per cent of the district's workforce over a twelve-month
period. As a hunch.

A huddle of pedestrians was forming up ahead at a crossroad;
no one willing to dodge through the traffic. Jayna hung back
from the patient crowd and looked into a corner antiques shop.
Why, she wondered, did people want to own these things? Not

for their utility. She wrinkled her nose at the clashing display of chairs, lace, jewelry, ceramics. An attempt to grasp rarity? Or a search for original forms, a search for the beginnings of things? Now *that* she found intriguing, something she could appreciate. She turned away from the shop front and smiled. A new line of research—sales at auction rooms, guide prices—purely because she'd changed her routine, taken a new route to work. A little tame, but a start.

As she crossed the junction, however, she sensed at the back of her mind something shouting for attention from her wildcat research—smell, taste, and olfactory signaling. She raised its status.

———

"Hi Jayna," said Dave. "You're into pigeons, too."

"I usually feed them on a Monday after work but I've changed my routine."

"Technically, they're pests."

"Who decides that, I wonder?" she said, almost to herself. She saw his quizzical look.

Undaunted, he said, "You're quite the animal lover, aren't you?"

"Pigeons are not animals. They're birds."

"I know that. It's just a figure of speech. I'm not totally stupid, you know."

"Sorry. I didn't mean that. I'm being pedantic. It's a common fault in…"

"I've noticed."

She tore another strip of crust from her sandwich. "You'll regret that at lunchtime," said Dave. She offered a piece of the crust to him. He took it from her palm and threw it as though throwing a stick for a dog. She laughed, and threw the remaining crumbs.

"Let's walk down together," he said.

"Come on, then. Let's not be late."

He strode through the pigeons. "My grandfather told me that his father could remember when all these parks were like tiny lungs sprinkled across the city. I liked the idea of that."

She didn't pursue this line of conversation. But it did remind her of the statements she had read in his personnel file:

David Madoc
Age: 27
Status: Organic
Residence: Enclave W3
Length of service: 7 years
Progression: Door greeter, boardroom attendant, archivist assistant
Potential for advancement: Capped

The subsidiary notes in his file revealed that his grandfather had been an academic before losing his job for the falsification of expense claims. The slippery slope, she thought.

"Olivia likes you, doesn't she?" said Jayna.

"Well, I'd never have my job in the public sector."

"So how did it come about?"

"I used to get the boardroom ready for big meetings and I suggested she buy some display books about *Jesse Recumbent*. I sourced them for her."

"That was you? I've seen them."

"Anyway, soon after, she moved me to Archives. That caused a stink."

"What happened?"

"Hester objected. But you know Olivia, didn't care what anybody said."

They passed a coffee house and she looked back at the office workers queuing to buy their cinnamon specials and pastries. "Smells good, hey?" said Dave. "Beyond me, unless the honey's selling well."

"Beyond my allowance, too. So, tell me, how did you end up keeping bees?"

"I wanted a better sideline. I used to buy and sell old books, still do now and then. But all along I was angling for the janitor's job at my flats. Took me three years to get it." He could see she didn't follow his drift. "If you get the janitor's job you get sole access to the roof. All you have to do is clean the stairwell, report any maintenance problems, check and clean the solar collectors."

"Does it pay well?"

"Nothing. The whole point is you *get* the *roof.* That's why people want the job. They use the roof to run a small business, like me and my bees."

"But why bees?"

"My grandmother had beehives before I was born and I always liked her stories about drones and giant swarms. It's a wonder I slept."

"And," she hesitated, "how far do they fly?" She remembered Hester's remark.

"I can't tag them." They both laughed. "But they can fly up to six miles from the hive. I think they collect pollen from the shuttle line embankments but they can easily reach the citrus groves. I like to think I'm flying with them." He flushed.

"Why would you want to do that?"

"You should see where I live."

"I'd like to."

"No, you wouldn't. Believe me."

"I'm serious. I'd like to."

"Are you allowed out? What's the set-up?"

"Yes, of course I'm *allowed out.* I just don't have much free time so I have to plan very carefully."

"How do you mean?"

"Well, if I want to attend events in the Entertainment Quarter, go to the Repertory Domes, I can only go at the weekend because

I don't have time on weekday evenings. Lights out at seven-thirty. I'm asleep by eight."

"What? That's outrageous."

"It's only unusual to you. You remember Frank? He could remain alert until much later. He could keep going until nine."

"That's bad enough. So what about the weekends? What will you do tomorrow?"

"I spend Saturday and Sunday mornings in my room, just processing. Some of my friends go to their offices but because Mayhew McCline is usually closed I tend to allocate particular tasks for the weekend."

"So your weekend afternoons are free?"

"Yes. I have lunch in our canteen and then I go out. Except this Sunday afternoon. We're holding a backgammon championship against the neighboring C6 rest station, which should be fun."

"Well, you certainly know how to enjoy yourself."

She looked towards and beyond him catching their reflection in the lime-tinted windows of New Broadcasting House. Her dream splashed into her mind. "*Sarcasm*," she said. "The use of bitter or wounding, especially ironic, remarks. Am I right?"

"I guess so. But the question is: do you feel offended?"

"I don't feel angry. That's probably outside my repertoire."

"Then what?"

"I think sarcasm is usually intended to demean a rival. Why would you want to do that?"

"Ah, come on. Don't take me so seriously. You should reply with an equally sarcastic remark."

"Like…? At least, Dave…" She wasn't sure about this. "At least I have the intellect to play something more challenging than draughts."

His facial muscles stitched pain. "A bit fucking close to the bone, Jayna. But good, a good retort."

As they entered the Grace Hopper Building, Jayna's fast-track processing on all-things-olfactory reached a set of conclusions. She turned to Dave. "Sorry. Didn't mean to be brutal. I'll try better next time." And she smiled sweetly with her eyes and her mouth.

She culled the key points:

The neural systems for smell and taste are separate but the sensations of flavors and aromas often work together. Flavor comes from food molecules that enter the nasal passages.

What came next was more intriguing:

The olfactory system is the most primitive sensory system because of its very early development in the evolutionary chain. Unlike the other senses, the olfactory sense has links through a back door to ancient areas of the brain.

In more detail:

Olfactory signals follow several pathways to different brain structures in the olfactory cortex, an area that evolved before those cortical areas of the brain associated with consciousness. This olfactory cortex lies at the bottom surface of the brain and has connections to the limbic system (hippocampus, amygdala, and hypothalamus), which is important in emotional states and in memory formation. Odor messages also go to conscious cortical centers, via the thalamus, where identification of the odor takes place. In other words, odor signals trigger emotional responses in the ancient areas of our brain before our conscious cortical areas can identify the smell.

And, specifically:

Illness and accidents can result in disorders. Less frequently, the olfactory system is affected by genetic traits. Hyperosmia is a heightened sense of smell. Anosmia is the inability to smell, which can be general or specific to one odor, though sufferers retain some sense of taste.

At her work array, she refocused and read her latest messages: Hester requested Jayna's comments on the final draft of Olivia's forthcoming paper for the Royal Society of Arts, which Jayna herself had ghostwritten. Benjamin wanted her to observe a contracts meeting with their public relations agency and then write a summary with recommendations.

No problem. Olivia's RSA paper would slot between her own priorities: find more hydrogen factors, investigate anosmia, and some digging around at the Institute of Forensic Accountancy. Exactly why had Nicole's time-keeping gone awry? Finding the answer, Jayna realized, would demand invasive maneuvers; serious risk-taking. So, as a precaution, she made a number of downloads on tax evasion prosecutions, which she reckoned would mask her true intentions. Then she searched for a path into the IFA's internal comms, keeping an eye on the time.

Eventually she infiltrated the IFA through the Metropolitan Police Department's Statistics Division. It was circuitous, but with her current access rating she knew she could slip through with little risk of detection. But just as she dipped into IFA's comms, Benjamin called her to his office.

————

"A couple of things, Jayna. You've approached Warwick University for progress reports on current research into olfactory disorders. What's that about?"

She feigned a bored sigh but her pulse leaped to 135 beats a minute. "It's going to be very time-consuming, Benjamin, if I have to justify all my lines of investigation." She decided to lower the pitch of her voice to mask an irregularity.

"I'm curious. I just want to understand how you work."

"The way I work is complex."

"Yes, and that's why you're here. Indulge me."

"Well, it's an established fact, isn't it, that diet has a causative link with hypertension and anti-social behavior?"

"Yes, and now we have urine alerts for dietary—"

She cut him off. "Not everyone has bathroom detection. Certain types of criminal behavior are on the increase among organics. So I decided to investigate the underlying urges that might cause these people to eat inappropriate foods. Hence, the smell and taste uploads. You see, in most of my investigations I'm propelled by my own curiosity. I make the retrievals instinctively, almost impulsively, once I have a line of thought."

"Hmm…I'm more selective, can't handle the same volumes of data. I have to be far more strategic." Benjamin raised his index finger towards his face and kneaded the flesh of his chin. He looked beyond Jayna, lost in private thought.

"You said you had a couple of things…"

"Yes." He stared at her, then remembered. "I considered your request. I'll let you visit a few people at home. Two conditions."

"Okay."

"I want you to visit only Mayhew McCline staff."

"I don't really know anyone outside Mayhew McCline."

"And I want to restrict this to two visits initially. Then we can review what you've gained from the exposure. I suppose you could visit me. I live close to the center."

"Yes? When?"

"Not this weekend. How about next Saturday?"

"So soon?"

"Why not? Let's say two o'clock if that fits your schedule. We'll have a barbecue."

Jayna's eyes widened. *What's his home like? Will his daughter be there? Is Benjamin a different person away from the office? Does he have a happy family? What will he put on the barbecue?* "Oh! Thank you, Benjamin. How kind of you."

"Get my address from the personnel files."

"I don't have access," she said, abruptly.

"Ask Eloise, then."

It was purely a precaution, she thought, as she left Benjamin. She'd only dipped into the personnel files. Not really worth asking permission. She wouldn't misuse the information. Why would she? Just avoided embarrassments. She'd learned that Craig had taken special leave last year when his marriage disintegrated. She knew that Dave was excluded from implantation and that Eloise had late implantation. And the recruitment files were interesting, too. Tom hadn't worked more than eighteen months for any employer over the past twelve years. Even with that record, Benjamin had been obliged to offer Tom a massive inducement to join Mayhew McCline.

Arriving back at her work array, she immediately resumed sifting through two months of IFA interdepartmental communications. She homed in on obvious keywords: *Nicole, recall, absence.* New keywords then emerged: *investigator, Barry*, and the surprisingly common double occurrence of *sick* and *bastard*.

All was now clear.

Nicole had formed a relationship with a man called Barry. He worked at the IFA in maintenance and cleaning services. That is, Nicole had formed an intimate relationship with an organic male. Strange! Jayna detected outrage in the communication streams. Not only had Nicole violated her protocols but apparently she had also shown appalling taste. Jayna found no official reason for her recall and it seemed only a handful of people within the IFA knew about her *cavortings with Barry in the broom cupboards.* Senior colleagues expressed bemusement that the organic could be sexually interested in a simulant but they inferred that Barry was *too thick* to realize what a *sick bastard* he was. Nevertheless, it appeared he had been dismissed with a payout from the Constructor to keep his mouth shut.

Jayna felt herself slump. She couldn't compete with that; Nicole had gone too far. And what had prompted her? Simulants didn't do sex.

A final exploratory foray unearthed a statement by the organic Barry.

How careless of them to leave that lying around. But she couldn't dwell on Barry's version of events; time was pressing. She withdrew from the IFA data, dusting her path, laying false trails, creating diversions, and finally she was back in friendly territory. Her heart was thumping.

Immediately, she prioritized her studies for Mayhew McCline and spent the rest of her working day weaving through official and unofficial texts, dispatching requests for clarifications, proposing hypotheses, and conducting tests through mathematical models; rejecting, refining, reiterating. She compiled a progress statement and dispatched it to Benjamin.

———

The communication from Dave was short and achingly sweet: *Would you like to meet up tomorrow afternoon?*

Jayna made no reply. She deleted the message from the entire Mayhew McCline system—a rigorous exercise that resulted in her working ten minutes late. On the way out, she called into Archives. "Don't do that again," she said, and placed a paper note in front of Dave. She turned on her heel and left. Dave unfolded the note: *13:15 hours, Antiquarian Bookshop on Portland.*

———

Julie called by Jayna's room that evening. The atmosphere over dinner had seemed subdued.

"Am I disturbing you, Jayna?"

"No, but I'm pretty tired tonight."

"I won't keep you. Just wondered if you want to do anything tomorrow afternoon."

"Rather not make any firm plans, Julie." She had to invent something. "I may need to work some extra hours."

"More than your contracted hours? You know you can report them."

"I know. But I want some solid results for my boss. I'd like to see him doing well—become a vice president."

"He's not your responsibility."

"I know but I feel I owe him. It was largely his decision to take my lease. And if he gets promotion, I think I'll be there long term. I don't like the idea of being reassigned."

"Oh! Jayna. I hadn't thought of that possibility."

"I expect you have more job security in the state sector."

"Maybe. But I think you're worried about nothing."

Jayna yawned. "I'm definitely not worried."

"Well, anyway, let me know if you want to meet up tomorrow." And she left.

Jayna flopped back on her bed and kicked off her shoes. She could quite happily have slept there fully clothed. She decided she'd try that some time.

As she studied the cracks in her ceiling plasterwork, she re-enacted the day's events: her morning detour to work, meeting Dave in the park, her reckless incursion into IFA data, Dave's potentially incriminating message, her reply, and the revelation of Nicole and Barry stealing moments together among mop buckets and paper towels. *I tell yer, there's no difference.* It was right there in his fragmented verbal statement, made in answer to a string of questions from a panel of directors and a constructor's representative:

I saw Nicole most days around the place, in the corridors. She usually spoke to me. Nothing much, just "Hello!" or "How are you?"

She was polite and always smiled. Then we started having a bit of a banter…Yeah, I thought she fancied me. I know she did. Other women do, too…So what's the big deal?…What's the difference? I tell yer, there's no difference. That's a fact…Mind yer own fuckin' business. All right, she responded…It was her fault if she missed important meetings…Well, sack me! It's a shit job anyway.

Fascinating. But Jayna was none the wiser about Nicole's motivation. She hadn't attended any disciplinary meeting. She hadn't made a statement. She'd simply disappeared.

One thing Jayna did notice from IFA timesheets—a correlation between a small number of Nicole's absences and the company chauffeur's stand-down time. They'd missed that.

CHAPTER 6

There was no actual rule about sitting in the recliner but its intended purpose as an aid to deep thinking was clear. So, for the first time, Jayna abandoned the recliner, stretched out on the bed, shut her eyes, and launched her Saturday processing session. *Let's stir things up*, she said to herself. *A less rational, less pedantic interrogation of the data…see what happens.* Selecting a three-dimensional oceanic construct, she scattered her data sets with a sower's sweep, forcing random encounters within the data, lots of them. She added churning currents; they would shift the data sets during the session. Maybe too complex but worth a try. She dived into her virtual ocean, straight through the statistics on world hydrogen production. Absorbing the information in an instant, she reached towards a cluster of data sets below—electrical goods recycling, locations of community nuclear power plants, water purification costs—sifted, regressed, correlated, pushed aside. She swam down through a vast swarm of data lying near the base of her construct—transport profiles for Londoners and New Yorkers, fueling depots across the road and rail networks, hydrocarbon production and refinery capacity, rare earth prices. Pointing her fingertips to the surface, she floated up through the energy stocks and modeled each company's performance, searching for those with statistically significant, positive alphas—those that out-performed the market.

She opened her eyes—an hour and a half had passed—and rested her mind awhile. One more attempt. This time she plunged through Europe-wide data for car ownership, fuel types, manufacturers, dealerships, scrap prices. She glimpsed a near-perfect proposition. But it lay beyond her grasp.

Patience. Something will emerge soon.

Most of the residents had dispersed by the time Jayna reached the canteen for lunch. She bowed low over her soup and noticed a scattering of crumbs across the table and three water rings. Good: the others had been and gone.

As normal for a Saturday afternoon, she set out from the rest station towards the Entertainment Quarter. Two blocks along, however, she turned southwest into Portland Street. Automated road cleaners were slowly clearing and spraying the gutters, sucking debris from the pavements. Steeling herself against any loss of nerve, she resumed her ongoing study of the city streets: the pattern of paving slabs and kerbstones, the incidence of cracking, and the distribution of manhole covers and grids. But her thoughts still bolted ahead. *I do actually like Dave.* She swept her colloquialisms. *He wears his heart on his sleeve. That's it…he's emotional, raw. He's even slightly unpredictable; perfect for me. I can learn so much from him, if he lets me.*

The bookshop came into view and, as though she might otherwise turn tail, she made a rapid-fire commercial assessment. An unprepossessing frontage, shop floor area, say, of thirty square meters, a gross profit margin of between 10 and 15 per cent of turnover, depending on their stock control, working capital, and liquidity ratios. Behind-the-wall earnings, most likely, many times the shop's turnover. The bookshop itself was a brand-building operation, she guessed…a myriad of unseen trading operations generating the bulk of the profits, and hence shareholder dividends, related to less exciting products delivered from warehouses located at transport hubs…

And now she stood at the shop entrance. Judging by the restricted opening hours, Jayna decided the shop assistant must be a simulant of the Frank or Freda variety, no doubt stuffed full of data on all things bookish—paper and binding quality, number of printings in each edition, number of issues incorporating minor changes, preferred editions, etc., etc. The perfect shop manager to deal with an erudite customer base.

Entering, she saw Dave at the far end of the shop but she turned to the female assistant. "May I browse?"

"Feel free. We have something for everyone—literature, classics, children's and illustrated, local history, travel and topography, decorative arts, things Japanese"—exactly, Jayna thought, a Freda— "and a section on regional maps printed mostly pre-1800…"

Dave guessed that Jayna had deliberately ignored him and he played along. "Jayna. Hi! Thought I knew the voice."

"Hello, Dave. I didn't expect to see anyone I knew here. Do you come here often?"

He hid a broad smirk by looking down at his feet. For all her brains, she came out with some rubbish lines. Forcing the smile off his face, he looked up. "I bought a couple of books for Olivia from here. What about you?"

"Just passing; thought I'd look in." She selected a book at random, flicking the pages, settling on the imprint.

"Don't you love the smell of old books?" he said.

Jayna was a blank. What was he talking about? Of course. An olfactory signal—pleasant memories. She looked at the small book in her hands then turned her back to the assistant to shield their conversation. "Let's go to your place, Dave. How long will it take?"

"Err…it's five stops out from the terminus on Line 3." This was all moving a bit fast and his eyebrows were darting. "How long have you got?"

"I need to be back by five-thirty."

"Okay. That's do-able."

"You leave now ahead of me and I'll follow you in three minutes. Wait at the platform till you see me and I'll join you on the shuttle."

"What's the cloak and dagger for?"

"I'll explain later."

Slowly he returned his book to the shelf, making time to think. "You look a bit too tidy for my neighborhood. I'll give you my top shirt when we meet up."

"All right. Now say 'goodbye' to me and go. Please."

He complied in a roundabout way partly for Freda's benefit. "Look, Jayna, I'm sorry. I have to rush. Great to see you, though." He leaned towards her—tilting his head twenty-five degrees from the vertical—moved his face towards her right cheek and placed his mouth against her skin. Simultaneously, he grasped her right upper arm and pulled her towards him; she pitched a half step forward, off balance. He pressed his mouth more firmly against her cheek. He released her. "Let's meet up soon." And he headed off.

She didn't think. She simply preserved the impression; his mouth on her face, his hand on her arm. And she held on to his smell. She waited. Waited. But no memories were triggered. Jayna couldn't work out why she liked the smell of his hair, his skin. This was something very simple; too basic for words. Only a shadow of Dave's touch remained. As she stared at the open book in her hands, she predicted that whenever she thought of this encounter she would always recall this little book. She flicked the pages, lifted the book, and inhaled molecules of old ink and paper. That too. She'd remember that.

———

Striking southwards, she tried to conjure images of Dave's life in the enclaves. And because the evidence of her eyes might later obliterate these imaginings, she decided to fix her mind-images—his street, his apartment, his belongings, his beehives. She could test her reality gap. But beyond the images, what else? Could she and Dave become so familiar and so totally at ease in one another's company, if she visited him often, got to know his neighbors well enough to pass conversation, if she and Dave shopped for groceries, walked through his local park on Sunday afternoons...Could they become the very best of friends? She imagined one possible future: *he's meeting me at the shuttle station and I'm waving, he's walking towards me, we're holding hands and walking through the streets together...we're drinking coffee at a pavement café.*

Leaving the commercial district, she walked along the glass-walled buildings of the sprawling university complex. The pavements widened and the dense canopies of whitebeam gave intermittent shade to the weekend pedestrians. Relegated, she thought, these whitebeam; just a form of sunblock now. But, once upon a time, they were the stuff of industry—the cogs, literally! As the sun flashed at her each time she strode out of the shade, it seemed the trees and sunlight conspired to send a message. For she made a firm decision to do more of this—take more walks through the city. Only, in future, she would walk without purpose, finding new places by chance. She passed two young women lying like bookends along a low wall, head to head; the space around them filled with chatter and shrill laughter. Luxury. Empty time.

Out in the open, she crossed the no-man's-land in front of the terminus. What were the chances, she wondered, of meeting someone from Mayhew McCline? And what would she tell them? Part of the truth: she'd been modeling the transport sector on and off for six months and not once had she traveled down a shuttle line. Anyway, if she had to, she could justify visiting Dave. Benjamin had given her clearance, of a kind.

Dave watched from the platform and held his over-shirt in his hand. Seeing Jayna approach, he stepped onto the waiting shuttle. She followed. There were nine other passengers in the compartment and Dave led her to a bench seat at the far end. The carriage was more utilitarian than she had expected: stripped down metal, no livery, wooden slatted seats, windows that opened manually, no air-conditioning.

"So what was all *that* about?" said Dave.

"I don't want anyone to know I'm meeting you."

"Why should the shop assistant matter? What's the problem?"

"I don't know for sure, Dave, but I don't think it would go down too well at the office. And the shop assistant was a simulant so if anyone asked questions she'd have perfect recall."

"It's your weekend. It's nobody else's business."

"They wouldn't see it like that."

"They don't fucking own you."

"No. Not quite. Well, yes, they do really."

The carriage juddered. They looked out as the shuttle gathered speed and within half a minute they were flying noiselessly away from the city center. The buildings blurred; she hunted for a recognizable feature. It made her eyes hurt. So she relaxed and tried to absorb the visual cacophony. And, this way, she sensed that the built forms were gradually changing in character from large bulks with shiny, reflective surfaces to smaller, less dazzling blocks with irregular rooflines; more complexity and more greenery. She grasped she was witnessing the compactness and semi-structured order of the suburbs. Despite the shuttle's speed, it was apparent that security wires lined the tracks.

At the precise moment this realization crystallized, the shuttle burst into a landscape so unrestricted that she gasped. An almost unreachable horizon, a high blue sky stretching across the entire landscape. She placed her hand flat against the window, for she wanted to stand out there, alone amid the giant discs of green and yellow that lay squat and unbounded on chocolate brown soils. She wanted to stand out there and feel the size of the planet through her feet. This was the first time she had appreciated—through the kind of revelation only granted, she now realized, to a witness—that the Earth really did curve, but so slightly. She felt less than tiny. She felt like a negative presence; a scratch of an entity on the skin of a planetary body.

The circular fields' bright colors grayed towards the horizon. These were the irrigated expanses of Outer Manchester, at one time a rain-fed region for cereals and livestock. Now, crops sprang to attention only at the command of overhead gantries with their clouds of water droplets. The discs gave way to endless, fuzzy lines etched across the bare earth as though the farmers were primarily tasked with an empirical study in perspective.

"The vineyards," she said.

"The olive farms lie south of here. And the citrus groves are farther west, closer to where I live," said Dave.

"It's beautiful."

"I know," he said. "But way out of reach."

She turned to him. "What do you mean?"

"It's a business; no room for day-trippers."

Facing forward again, she detected something low and shapeless emerging through the heat haze. Even as they sped closer she discerned no punctuations; no towers, no spires, no cranes. This had to be the first enclave, she thought. The shuttle slowed towards the station and the new urban landscape became a reality. No clear signs of economic activity, no factories, only three small warehouses on a siding; minor distribution depots, she supposed. She caught sight of street lights but no vehicles, and monotonous blocks of low-rise housing units, four to six storeys high, clearly set out on a grid pattern, untidy with clothes hanging from balconies, which—as far as she could make out—were largely relegated to household storage. Several balconies, however, were boarded up, possibly to make additional rooms. She wondered if the architects for these miserly buildings had sketched patio furniture for these ostensibly desirable indoor-outdoor spaces.

The shuttle pulled into the station. Functionality laid bare; no advertising hoardings, no wrought-iron squirls hinting at former glory days. No romance had ever been connected to this place, she thought. "It's not what I expected."

"I did warn you."

"Yes, but are all the enclaves like this? Aren't there any parks?"

"Parks? You're thinking of the inner suburbs. We've passed those. Our shuttles don't even stop there. We're pushed out to the enclaves as fast as possible."

"I know…but I didn't realize the enclaves looked like this." She sighed. "I guess I didn't translate the data too well."

At each shuttle stop, the urban vista remained a monochrome. But the intervening countryside transformed into a sea of citrus—a whispered reminder, she thought, of the country's wild and wooded past, when great oaks were felled and carved into giants just like Olivia's *Jesse*.

"Put the shirt on, Jayna. We'll be there in two minutes."

She felt her throat tighten. Her breathing became shallow. Her imagination had failed her. Already the reality gap was huge. *I should peer between the lines of data; interpolate rather than extrapolate. I could have deduced something closer to the truth. I simply wasn't looking for it.*

CHAPTER 7

Station Five: two concrete platforms, a concrete pedestrian bridge, no platform buildings, no personnel; only the sound of children, screeching, beyond the station perimeter wall. Dave and Jayna walked through an unmanned gateway, out onto a vast hardstanding, bare except for the faded markings of parking bays and the scattered intrusions of lusty flowering weeds. She traced the faint painted lines with her steps and called to Dave above the clamor of the children, "Did your family own a car?" He shook his head. She recalled one of those barren facts: private car ownership in the enclaves, in the ten years following the Major Relocations, fell from an average of 30 per cent to zero.

"Until I was seven years old, we went on day-trips with the Stephensons, family friends. But they had to sell their car."

The children's game-playing hurtled jaggedly across the open ground; Jayna kept her eyes on them. "The car…too expensive to run?" she said, distracted. The nearest housing blocks stood three hundred meters away. Where exactly were they heading? The children's chasing game swerved towards them. Instinctively she side-jumped closer to Dave.

"It's okay, they won't bother us." He laughed. "Only kids." But Jayna stuck close. They were wild and dusty looking, and shod in the flimsiest of flip-flops—perilous! They yelled at one another while executing some demented game elaborated with ropes and multi-colored, hand-painted sticks. It did *not* seem like fun-play to her. There were taunts. Were there two separate groups involved, three even? In the midst of their play, she suspected, small terrors were being meted out.

"Yeah, the car had to go. They had good jobs in the Civil Service but, first, Mrs. Stephenson was downgraded to menial work and, soon after, the same happened to her husband." One boy slammed headlong into the ground and three other children—two boys and a girl, as far as Jayna could make out—ran towards him with raised sticks. But the boy scrambled on his belly for his own stick and lashed out threatening to strike their ankles. "Then they were forced out of the Civil Service completely. Good payouts, apparently. But it was tough for them; all those aspirations. You know—" his mood lifted "—we used to drive south towards Shropshire and take a picnic. It was fantastic. *They* had the car. *We* paid for the fuel. And my parents had a brilliant picnic set. It was my grandparents' originally; the real thing—matching crockery, heavy cutlery, and glasses. We felt like minor royals." The kids parted into two unbalanced tribes to find their way around Dave and Jayna but he seemed not to notice. "We'd spread two rugs and set everything out. Absolute magic. All day in the fresh air just messing about."

The sticks were clashing and she could see chips in the paint-work—old scars, or notches. "I don't quite follow." She shifted around the back of Dave to keep away from the main group of kids. "If the Stephensons had good jobs, responsible jobs, why didn't they get bionic status automatically?"

"Same as my family. Something dodgy in the background, on her side I think. And he was ruled out by association."

How much did Dave know about his grandfather's fall from grace, Jayna wondered? Did his grandfather deny the allegations? Did he have a good lawyer? His family paid a high price if he didn't.

As they neared the housing blocks, she realized they were heading for the widest street leading away from the car park. The children's screams gave way to a ruckus emanating from farther down the street where a crowd jammed the space between the buildings. A young man, wearing shorts and rubber boots, pedaled slowly towards them on a creaking, three-wheeled cycle pulling a lopsided trailer loaded with rubbish. He stood alternately on each pedal using his total body weight to jerk the cycle forward.

"What's going on, Dave? And where's he going with the rubbish?"

"It's our Saturday market. You'll like it. And he's a freelance taking waste to the generators on the eastern side of town. It's usually down-wind." They both laughed. The bike stammered past and they covered their faces with their hands.

"I live up this street, off to the left. In fact…it's a great spot, courtesy of our employer."

Dave walked with a swagger, she noticed; a man on home ground. "Meaning?"

"I'm high on the priority list because I work for Mayhew McCline." She looked uncertain. "Works like this, Jayna: the best flats go to people working for top companies like Mayhew's—they pay towards the subsidies. Next in the pecking order are public sector operatives. Outside of that, it's a free-for-all and when it's rotation time it's total chaos: pavements everywhere piled with furniture being moved in or moved out. Looks like the entire enclave has been lifted up and shaken out."

"Who's actually involved in the rotations?"

"If you don't have any priority, there's a standard long-term lease from the housing department and the quality's poor to mid-dling. Or you can opt for ten years' participation in lottery accommodation, flats are rotated every two years on a rolling program. But it's not a real choice. And people get really mad—"

"I've seen reports on the housing riots."

"Right. It's fuck-stupid…" She prickled. "It's a game; everyone hoping for a better deal next time. There *are* a few good flats but not many. People build their hopes up…Mind you, when I say *good* I only mean they're a bit bigger or closer to the station."

Street vendors had set out their produce on cloths and plastic sheeting laid at the pavement edge: a box of over-ripe fruit, an array of battered household gadgetry. But most street sellers were displaying just a handful of items, and the smallest display was a single pair of men's slippers placed on a piece of brightly patterned cloth. The vendor, an elderly woman, sat on a stool behind her offering.

"It's the scrag-end, here. The only decent things are over there—the booksellers." He led her across.

"Bit different from Portland Street," she said. No stalls as such. The booksellers had purloined a waist-high wall that extended from a block of flats. The wall separated the street from the block's recycling bins but for market day it was transformed into a long bookshelf, spines facing the sky; perfect ergonomics for browsers.

"*Better* than Portland. If you make a purchase you can also do a swap. And that way the stock's always changing."

"That's smart."

He grinned. "You can't teach much to these guys."

She walked along the line of books lightly touching them with her hand. Most of the spines were damaged. "What kind of books do you buy, Dave?"

"Anything, really. I've had a couple of books about bees from here. They were handy. Otherwise, I look out for old comics…and those motivational books, always good for a laugh."

"Perhaps I'll try one."

"Come on. We'll take the next right, and then left. The parallel street is better."

They veered off and, approaching the next turning, she looked aloft and laughed. "What's this, Dave?"

"The start of Clothing Street."

A gigantic sheet of pink fabric flapped lazily in the gentle breeze, way above their heads. It was strung between the top floors of the buildings on either side of the street. He guided her towards the right and they walked along stalls selling unpackaged clothes piled high. "This leads down to the food market but stay close: it's easy to get separated."

Any notion of personal space evaporated as they edged along the stalls. She felt buffeted as people crossed haphazardly from one side of the street to the other, from one stall to the next. The traders bawled out as though no one would air any money without a performance; they cajoled, wooed, and raised laughter here and there. Jayna noticed the mismatched tables—old doors supported on stacks of battered crates. Fit for purpose, she thought. They stopped near a long stretch of tables where women, mostly, were congregating, elbowing for position. One woman held up a child's shirt by the shoulder seams, another stretched the waistband of a skirt. Several women waved garments and shouted their offers. Another woman threw a jacket back to the tangle in apparent disgust at the price and moved on.

"It's chaotic." She shook her head gently. "Where do all these clothes come from, Dave?"

"It's recycled. The cheapest stuff comes from the enclaves but the best is collected from the suburbs."

"None of it's new?"

"No one really wears new. But over there, see? Those traders take clothes apart and remake them. Want to look?"

Jayna was already one step ahead of him. "Do you ever buy anything from here?" she called over her shoulder.

"Now and then, just a re-make shirt or T-shirt."

Fewer items were on sale here, which proved their relative worth. But everything looked oddly dysfunctional. On any one garment there were mismatched buttons, sleeves of different material. She winced at the sight of a mock-fur collar stitched to the neckline of a striped cotton shirt; nauseating, disparate things being forced together. Looking at the prices she mused on the labor costs of unpicking and re-sewing. She guessed the cost of the raw materials. "Do traders pay much for these stalls?" she said.

"There's a hefty license fee paid upfront and then a daily charge."

"Who does the making?"

"Migrants, freelancers."

"Makes me feel incredibly plain. Not sure I like any of it."

"Try something on." He smiled. "No harm in that." She picked up a cap. It seemed safe; it wouldn't touch her skin if she were careful. "Go on, put it on." He laughed. "There's a mirror."

She stood, cap in hand, and looked in the tatty reflector beside the stall but she couldn't bring herself to put the cap on. So Dave took it from her hand and, standing in front of her, knees slightly bent so he could look straight at her eyes, placed the cap on her head. He took it off, pushed her straight hair behind her ears, and replaced it. "That's better." He lifted her chin with the side of his index finger and stood aside. She shuddered, failing to recognize her own reflection.

"What do you think?" he said.

The cap was made of army camouflage but the peak was fluorescent lemon with beads sewn on the underside. She took it off, and then put it back on. And she repeated this twice, to the point where she attracted looks from other shoppers. "Dave?"

"It's great."

"I don't feel right. I can't recognize who I am."

He laughed. "It's called *dressing up.*"

"But what does the cap say about me?"

"I guess it says you're…different."

"I don't need a cap to tell me that, do I?"

"You might want to tell other people."

"What would that achieve?" With a sense of relief she put the cap aside and they moved on. They yielded willingly to the crowds allowing themselves to be nudged and pushed against one another as they inched closer to the food market. They came to an intersecting street and Dave put his arm around her waist to help steer her across. She leaned into him, hoping to replicate the shock she'd felt in the bookshop.

"Clothing Street," she said. "I love it. It's so…random."

An old man pulling a handcart barged his way through the dawdling shoppers, shouting, "Aside! Aside!" He forced Dave and Jayna to make way. Dave pulled her arm and they fell in behind the cart—the old man thus easing their way to the end of street.

They emerged into the open food market. Heat and citrus mingled in the air. Did heat have a smell, she wondered? Or was it just the dust…? The full-on sounds that reverberated off the walls of Clothing Street dissipated now into a broad hum; the sun seemed to burn off the higher-pitched cries. Jayna rushed towards the stalls clustered under a grubby patchwork of multi-colored plastic—a makeshift canopy that shielded the vendors' wares and trapped the aromas in unruly combinations.

"There's something mixed in with the citrus…" she said. "But I can't name it."

Dave smiled. "I know what you mean. It's overpowering… might be fennel…Come on, let's cut across this corner of the market. We're nearly there."

The plastic canopies cast exotic hues across the shoppers' faces, deepening Jayna's sense of claustrophobia. He was right: a sensory overload. And although the smells were intoxicating, she could see that none of the produce—the blood oranges, cherries, apricots, grapefruit, and, yes, fennel—was prime quality. It was all either misshapen or beyond its best, in good company with the piles of ill-favored Ugli fruit. Dave pushed between two artichoke and asparagus stalls towards a narrow alleyway. The upper windows on the south-facing side were shuttered against the mid-afternoon sun. She thought of the flats' occupants, denied the cooler temperatures of the shaded lower floors. Maybe the stronger breeze up there offered some compensation.

Two hundred meters farther along, Dave turned abruptly into an open stairwell. At this point, she realized she had not seen a single pavement café since they arrived in the enclave.

"I'm on the top floor; it gets hot but it's quieter…and I sleep under a mozzy net on the roof in mid-summer."

The muddy colors of the outside world poured into the stairwell through windowless openings, creating an impressive monotone relieved only by the marks made by people journeying up and down the stairs, a history recorded in scratches, scrapes, and the occasional gouge, traced now by Jayna's fingertips. Dave paused on the fourth-floor landing and, half a flight below, she looked up at him. "I'd love to see the hives."

———

Out on the roof, they were struck by the full onslaught of the sun. The air was supercharged by the urgency of the bees. She felt diminutive, drowned in Dave's grubby protection suit and veiled hat. But despite being kitted out, she stood close to him, her gloved hand touching his bare arm. "Won't they sting you?" she said.

"Nah! I'll be okay. We'll keep our distance."

She kept eyeing the edge of the building. The perimeter wall was lower than knee height. "Do they know you, your smell?"

"Shouldn't think so. They're too busy to notice."

"Why keep bees, though? Why not grow vegetables?" Because it occurred to Jayna that vegetables could not chase her to the building's edge. She nudged into him again.

"Bees need very little attention. And no one's going to nick them."

"I didn't think of that."

"And the honey is easy to sell. So is the beeswax. What's more, nothing goes off." There were eight hives, closely spaced. Some in the shadow of a large water tank. "I built the hives myself."

She looked across to the surrounding buildings. Solar collectors covered a third of their roof spaces but they had little else in common. A maze of clothes hung from lines on the nearest block and on another roof there appeared to be plants trained on trellises. Others had contraptions of pipes and metal cylinders. Dave followed her gaze. "They're all businesses run by the janitors. Not many of them have the nerve to keep bees." He laughed. "And I'm not telling them how easy it is." He brushed a persistent bee from his face.

The bees were in a frenzy, diving in and out of the small entrance to each hive.

"It feels so free up here," she said.

"I doubt the bees think so. One bee makes less than half a teaspoon of honey in its lifetime." He turned and cranked open the metal door that gave access, down the stairs, to his top-floor landing. "Come on. You've seen it. It's too hot."

"Does everyone want to be a janitor?" she said as she followed him down.

"Yeah, there's plenty competition. But you have to stay in one place for a long time to be eligible. That rules out everyone taking lottery accommodation. Then you need good references. And you have to present a good business plan for your roof enterprise. They don't want the space wasted."

"So what are those other businesses?"

"You saw the laundry next door. Then, there are hydroponicas. Some are gardens; you pay a membership fee for so many visits per month. Rabbit or pigeon breeding, that kind of thing." He stored the protective gear in his janitor's cupboard.

"Could you sell your bee business? The goodwill, I mean."

"No. Not legally anyway. Why do you ask?"

"Just curious. Wondered how it compared with bigger business."

"Well, for a start, I sell honey and beeswax mainly at Mayhew McCline so there's no goodwill to sell. But an established bee colony should be worth something."

"Could you sublet the business, informally?"

He spoke quietly: "It happens, but you'd lose the roof if you were found out. People get jealous, Jayna, so it's best to keep within the rules. I keep the stairwell spotless so no one can complain— there's always someone ready to snatch the job. Anyway, I don't want to sublet. I like having the business." He took a single key from his pocket and unlocked his apartment door. He looked back over his shoulder at her. "Don't expect much. I didn't know you'd be coming so…"

"I don't live in luxury myself."

No hallway; they stepped directly into his living space. The room was spartan. She sensed this before Dave had even opened the shutters—the sound of his footsteps crossing the room seemed sharp and clear, not the muffled sounds she'd expect in a chaotic room. As light flooded the space, she hunted down details and the revelation, coming almost instantly, was unexpected. It was a small room replete with alignments. If he gave the impression at Mayhew McCline that he craved disruption, there was no evidence of any such tendency at home: three pans hanging in size order from a wooden batten, kitchen and bathroom items strictly segregated on opposite sides of the steel sink, a shelf of perhaps two dozen books standing vertically with two sets laid on their sides acting as efficient props. She detected that Dave was…*resolute* and, more than likely, he lived alone; no glaring inconsistencies or any indication of a bland compromise. This was Dave's place, she reckoned, and it was organized to suit him alone.

"Well, this is it," he said.

"It's bigger than my room. And a cooking area. I'd love that. Though…I don't know how to cook." She smiled.

"I could teach you sometime."

"Could I choose the meal?"

Won over, he laughed. "Within reason. It would have to be fish or vegetable something." He removed two glasses from his sole wall cupboard and filled them with water from a covered jug.

Jayna sipped her tepid water; Dave bolted his back.

"Do you know how to make real coffee?" he said. She shook her head. "Okay. Watch this."

Once again he reached into the cupboard and brought forth the apparatus for his act of alchemy: a cast iron contraption, which he clamped to the wooden board that spanned between the sink and the external wall of the kitchen; two small straight-sided cups in lime green, which he sat on two off-white saucers—one slightly too small for the cup, and the other too large (which combination did she prefer, she wondered?); two teaspoons with robed figures for handles; and a small black plastic bag. One end of the bag was tightly rolled and secured with a metal clip. He released this clip, took Jayna's hands, and placed one upturned palm alongside the other, then poured whole coffee beans from the bag into her cupped hands. She reacted automatically, lifting the beans and lowering her face. Her action felt primeval. Here was a gesture performed over millennia, she could sense it, either in ritual or as a survival tactic. An image appeared to her: an early, hairy progenitor lifting water from a pool, the hand as receptacle.

Step by step, Dave revealed to Jayna the magic of converting these dry dark beans, already intensely aromatic, into a steaming, high-inducing drink. She absorbed the irregular rumbling and crushing sounds, so unlike the frantic and homogenous screamings of automated grinders. Later, she would play and replay in her mind these seductive, hand-iron-bean sounds in the solitude of her room. She would dissect the grindings, stretch the time-scales and try to match the individual sounds of destruction with step-changes in the level of fragrance. Devouring his every move, she recognized a well-rehearsed routine of precise individual movements. Breathless at the beauty of this process, she had to remind herself of the ritual's purpose—Dave was making the perfect cup of coffee, for her. As he poured near-boiling water onto the ground beans she allowed her gaze to shift from the swirling coffee, away from the focus of this endeavor, to the hands of the alchemist. And she recalled his affectionate gestures in the bookshop and felt giddy.

She tried to de-agitate her mind by comparing Dave's room with her own. He had a small sofa whereas she had a better entertainment console. He had a picture of the Earth taken from the Moon. She had interesting cracks on her ceiling, which she had mentally enhanced and colored to make a virtual series of 723 abstracts. And then, he had his shelf of books, whereas she had her stick insects.

They sat on unmatched chairs—cast-offs, she guessed, from Mayhew McCline—at a square table made from strips of recycled wood, sanded down. Some strips were wider than others and most had remnants of old paint trapped in divots. Dave held the sides of the table and his middle fingers teased the imperfections. She wondered if he'd made the table himself but before she could part her lips to ask, a small eddy of information swirled through her mind and throbbed for attention. She tried to stifle it but then let it surface. *Should I...?* Her foot began tapping. *Should I...act on this?*

"Why did you want to come here, Jayna?"

She picked up the robed figure and stirred her coffee, far too quickly. "I wanted to see a home."

He sat forward, took the teaspoon from her hand, and laid it back on the saucer. "And?"

She noticed, for the first time, the hairs on the back of his hand. "Yes, there is more. There are other reasons." She settled her eyes on her steaming coffee. Five major tones ranging from creamy brown to brown-brown, that is, a dark chocolate brown; a little world in itself, air bubbles popping and steam rising, a primordial swamp. "I want something *unexpected* to happen. Something outside my usual routine."

"Life's a bit boring?"

"It's not that. I think a change in routine might be helpful."

"In what way?"

"I have this idea…that I might be…less surprised by events. I think I'd make better predictions if I knew more about other people's lives, if I could feel for myself that things don't always happen as anticipated." She felt a tic under her right eye. "Not only that, maybe I'd be a little less…wooden. If that's the right word. And, that's not all."

"Go on."

She looked down into her coffee. "I also want to have a friend who I can visit at the weekend. Someone who isn't…well, who's completely normal."

He looked down, stirred the *crema* of his own coffee and shook his head. "No such thing. There's no normal." And he looked up at her. "Let's face it. The likes of Hester and Benjamin think *they* are the norm. They've made themselves the yardstick."

"Well, whatever you say, I'm certainly not normal. There are so many things I can't do, Dave. I don't even know what I'm missing."

"And what about me?" He slowly drank some coffee and set the cup gratingly on the too-small saucer. "I'm an organic. That was normal at one time. But I'm made to feel a freak." He leaned forward. "Look, Jayna, there are plenty of things I can't do either. Before implantation ever started, someone like me could have a real career, travel places. But I've got as far as I'll ever get at Mayhew McCline."

"You might be right."

He sat back. "You've seen my file, haven't you?"

"Yes, I have, Dave. Well, I'm not supposed…" And a silence sat between them.

"Well, now I know. Dave Madoc is not a special case. I'll have to keep my head down and toe the line if I want to keep this flat."

She liked the way he mixed his metaphors. Careless or carefree?

"Why did you never have an implant, Dave?" She wanted his version.

"I failed the genetic risk assessment at eighteen. No surprise. My maternal grandfather was expelled from his university post. I always knew that. But I'm eligible for late implantation— my parents were squeaky clean all their adult lives, model employees…"

"So?"

"I can't afford it. And I don't want to take a loan. And, in any case, I hate the whole idea."

"But why?"

"Too big a trade-off. I feel sorry for the poor bastards really. They're so fucking sensible all the time."

She smiled. Then caught herself. "Tom wasn't exactly sensible, was he? Swimming out into strong currents."

"He wasn't being stupid. It was a misjudgment."

"Anyway, Dave, you're already partly bionic."

"No, I'm not."

"Inoculated at birth? Protected from addictions and most diseases?"

"I didn't get any choice about that, did I?"

"Even so, you're not saddled with any inclination towards self-destruction—over-indulgence in drugs, alcohol, gambling. Look how safe it is for everyone now: hardly any crime. You've all been liberated. Implantation is the obvious next step."

"I just don't want it. To be honest, I *like* losing my temper now and then. I *like* sitting out all night on the roof and bunking off work the next morning. Once you take the implant, you're trapped. I've never heard of a bionic just dropping out, resigning their fancy job, and fucking off to the hills."

"Well, I can't see how they could survive in the hills. In any case, maybe some do go to the hills, Dave, and you don't know about it…Which hills are you talking about?"

"Hold on. I didn't mean the hills, literally. I mean *dropping out*, disappearing, living on the margins."

She hesitated. "There could be bionics living here in your enclave without you realizing who they are."

"I suppose so…I haven't heard of any."

"It's possible though."

They sat without speaking, each taking sips from their coffee.

"Jayna, let's face it. You've not much to worry about on the scale of things. You don't have to worry about money. You've got free housing, meals, clothes. And the best job in the company below director level. Am I right?"

"Yes. I know I have a good job and an easy life but I feel…I don't know…For one thing, someone's spraying yellow paint across the rest stations and writing *No* with an exclamation mark—four this week, including ours."

"Graffiti?"

"Is it?"

"They'll soon be picked up. Could be some crank worried about their job."

"Well, it's not just that. The fact is that my status is highly ambiguous." Dave burst into laughter but she persisted. "Please. I'm serious. I have no past and that seems to lessen all my rights. You know, at any moment I could be recalled and reinitiated. I'd be a blank slate again. Dave, I wouldn't know you if I fell over you in the street. And I wouldn't be interested in stick insects and wouldn't crave fresh coffee or fantasize about eating Singapore Style Rice Vermicelli…"

"Whoa! Wait there. Why would they want to recall you?"

She stood, took her cup to the sink, rinsed it and lay in gently on the wooden board. "I think there might be something wrong with me; a glitch." A faint shudder ran across her shoulders and she turned to face him. "It's happened to other simulants, and they've been taken back to the Constructor."

He studied her. "What's gone wrong with them?"

"Different things."

"Like?"

"Poor time-keeping, sneaking into restaurants, sexual liaisons."

He leaned back, lifted his hands to the back of his head, and pulled them forward, ruffling his hair as he did so.

"It's not supposed to happen," she said.

After a moment's silence: "Who else have you told about this?"

"No one. No one knows. No one knows I'm here. Not even my friends at the rest station. I haven't told anyone about what I'm doing or thinking."

"Better keep it that way. Let's hope the Constructor isn't watching you all. And don't raise any suspicions at work."

Taking his cup to the sink, he lowered his voice: "Bit of a risk coming here."

"I think I'm covered for today. I've got approval from Benjamin to visit Mayhew McCline staff and his conditions were woolly. He didn't rule anything out, though…Dave, I don't think you'd get into any trouble."

"I started it anyway."

She smiled, reluctantly. "I suppose."

"Look, you know, Jayna, don't you? You may not be able to do this again. It could be too risky."

"Don't say that."

He stood before her in his well-worn bleached out clothes and she couldn't help wondering if he was a shade underweight. How would he look if he upped his calories? Or was this his natural state? Maybe his parents had handed him a strong metabolism along with the suspect genes. She noted a sensation she'd felt two days ago when Lucas spilt the news of a second recall. She'd felt tense then, but this was stronger. She could feel her stomach muscles tensing and then relaxing and then tensing again. And she needed to swallow.

"Don't talk about risk," she said firmly. "I want to come here again." He didn't need further prompting. He leant down and kissed her cheek. She turned her face towards his and their mouths met.

His eyes closed; her eyes stayed open.

She laid her palm against his chest as if confirming their connection; a heartbeat. The forefingers of her other hand found the belt loops of his jeans. She tugged a little. *A fair start*, she thought, *but what happens next?* Dave's arms were around her. He didn't seem to be hurrying. They were still kissing; for how much longer? *I must be getting it all wrong. What else…?* She tried to unbutton his shirt and instantly felt the uncanniness of performing a familiar task with extraordinary clumsiness; she felt uncoordinated, realizing she'd never looked at how a button escaped its stupid buttonhole. He let go, stood back a step, and finished unfastening his buttons. He shrugged the shirt off his back. There seemed only one option— she'd simply copy him. She took off her shirt. He took off the rest of his clothes and chucked them aside. So she did the same. He laughed and she smiled. "Is this right?" she said.

"Absolutely." And for the next thirty-five minutes she explored the near-flawless body of this organic man, as he explored the perfect average-ness of this simulant woman. She trusted her earlier instinct and simply aped as many of Dave's actions as her physiology allowed. No need to think, she decided, this was purely physical. In time, it seemed her vigor as much as his impelled them through a cycle of gentleness followed by greed, followed by gentleness. And she felt safe.

————

A bee buzzed intermittently at the shutter slats, preventing Dave and Jayna from slipping into sleep. They lay on their sides facing one another, their skin catching the faint breeze that barely disturbed the solid heat of the room. Their eyes flicked open at random intervals.

There was something attractive, she mused, about Dave's mouth but she couldn't work out what it was. She traced the edge of his lips with her forefinger. It seemed to be a stone mouth, sculpted. His lips hardly broke the plane of his face. The mouth of a stoic, maybe.

She realized she was no longer tuned into the buzzing bee. Instead, she'd registered and was now following the blurred sounds of a conversation downstairs: a man and a woman. Their windows must be open, too, she thought. His voice, then her voice. His voice again, and her voice, higher and louder. Then a shout. "What's going on, Dave?"

He opened his eyes and kissed her. "They're just warming up. Picked a great time."

"What?"

"Every other weekend. They slowly wind one another up and then let rip. The record is three weeks without a blow-up." The two voices started to overlap.

"Don't you complain?"

"Not worth it. They'll wear themselves out." He kissed her again. "Try to ignore it." But she couldn't.

A child cried. "Oh Christ! The baby's joining in now," he said, exasperated.

Jayna sat bolt upright. "Why's the baby crying?"

"Just frightened. Doesn't like the shouting." The child's cry cranked to a warbling scream. Dave rolled onto his back.

"We must do something, Dave. Make them stop."

"It's okay. When *they* stop, the *baby* stops."

"I think they're hurting it."

"No. They're not. It sounds worse than it is. Babies always cry like that…no sliding scale."

"I don't believe…just listen." It was stomach churning.

"We can't do anything, Jayna."

She jumped up, hands over her ears. "It's horrible. I can't bear it." She turned to him. "We must go down and stop them, now." She grabbed her clothes from the floor. Before she could attempt to dress he took hold of her. The shouting and screeching ran up the walls, surrounding them. And something smashed. The woman's voice stretched to an even higher pitch, competing with the child's. "Dave?"

"It's okay. It will stop. I promise."

She pushed away from him. Her nails caught his shoulder, leaving two red slashes. "I'm going downstairs." But as she pulled on her shirt, the shouting ended. And a minute later the child stopped crying, just as Dave had said it would. He took her hand. She strained to hear.

Eventually she spoke: "How can you bear it, knowing it's going to happen again?" She moved aimlessly about the room. She found herself at the sink and leaned over, turned on the tap, and rinsed her face. He followed and placed his hand on her shoulder. But her thoughts were roaming far away. "Tom's children must be crying like that," she said with her face in her hands.

"Not like that, Jayna. It's not the same."

———

They dressed. She put on Dave's top shirt once again as he waited by the door. She hesitated, reluctant to step outside. "Time to go," she said, as if to herself.

He followed her down the first flight of steps and, as she turned for the second flight, the door opened to the downstairs flat. The couple stepped out. He was holding the child—asleep against his chest. Jayna froze.

"Hi, Dave. Going to introduce us?" said the woman.

He ignored the question. "Hi there. Where are you all off to?"

"Going for a stroll. It's blazing hot in there."

"Yeah, I heard."

And the couple laughed.

———

"How could you make a joke of it?" Jayna walked faster than necessary.

"Come on. Don't let them spoil things."

"The baby was screaming and now you're all laughing."

"There's no real harm done."

"You can't possibly know that."

They walked behind a wide-backed man who led a young boy by the hand. The boy could barely keep up; he progressed with a choppy mix of short walking and running steps. The boy tripped but the man kept him upright by pulling his arm upwards. Jayna heard the boy complain. The man gave a nasty, gratuitous yank to the child's arm.

"Why do you pretend it's all right?" she said.

They continued to the station without speaking. When the shuttle came within earshot, she removed the top shirt and handed it back to Dave. "We can't talk at work. You know that, don't you? And no messages either."

"So can we meet again?"

"I don't know. I have to think…"

Dave gently touched her arm but the sound of the fast-approaching shuttle obliged her to turn away.

He waved as the shuttle slid from the station. She didn't wave back. On the distant edge of the overgrown car park she caught a glimpse of two dogs—a male mounting a seemingly passive bitch. Different for people, she thought.

And now, she pushed all her confusion aside and reflected on the swirl of information that, earlier in the afternoon, over coffee, had set her a new challenge—one that, rightly or wrongly, she had taken up:

The sense of smell in mammals, including humans, is linked with the sex drive. Genetic dysfunction in the olfactory system can lead to sexual dysfunction among uninitiated adults. However, in adult mice, this dysfunction has been shown to spontaneously reverse once the mice have been introduced to sexual activity.

She was clear on the essentials even if the detail eluded her: the first simulants, the Franks and Fredas, were genetically manipulated to exhibit total anosmia, a complete loss of smell—one step, she guessed, in a complex strategy to disrupt the hypothalamic-pituitary axis—the aim being to destroy procreational instincts. More to the point, in advanced simulants such as herself, the degree of anosmia had been lessened to allow a greater degree of emotional development. *Hence, we* fit in *better at work.* But now she had a hunch: the Constructor had failed to optimize the degree of anosmia. Just like the lab mice, once the virgin simulant had experimented with sex, the sexual urge received a kick-start.

The enclave disappeared from view and her thoughts drifted. *Could I drop out? Should I run to the hills?* But, for once in her calculated life, she could divine no answer.

CHAPTER 8

On Sunday morning, Jayna made her breakthrough with the energy studies seemingly by accident. After days of effort, she found it oddly dissatisfying that her insight was precipitated during a momentary loss of focus. It occurred as she withdrew from the construct, as she floated back to the ocean's surface, when she had almost given up. A bit disappointing, she thought. Though it didn't really matter how she got there.

If everything stacked up, Benjamin and Olivia would be euphoric. And the timing was perfect—Mayhew McCline could push out the report just before the half-yearly staff appraisals. Jayna mapped out the next ten days:

Monday: request extended database searches.

Tuesday: complete extended research.

Wednesday: submit research findings to Benjamin in a Draft Energy Report for circulation and comment by board members.

Thursday: compile the responses.

Friday: submit Final Energy Report to Benjamin and Olivia for approval.

Monday next: report goes to production.

Tuesday next: check press releases.

Wednesday next: release the report, An Energy Investment Strategy, or some such.

On the basis of the data currently available, and as a result of Mayhew McCline's pronouncement on the subject next week, she reckoned that sales of in-vehicle hydrogen conversion systems would increase by between 10 and 15 per cent (a conservative range of values). Share prices for the makers of these complex systems would rocket. Somebody, somewhere, was going to make a great deal of money, she thought.

Pulling herself out of her recliner, she experienced a heaviness in her body, an ache in her back. She knew she must steady her pace, get plenty of sleep, stay alert. But she couldn't ease up too much. Standing by her window, she looked out towards Granby Row. Her east-facing room had lost its morning luminescence and Jayna felt the gaucheness of being indoors when the sun beat down just meters away. She assessed her next moves and assiduously re-ordered her research priorities:

One: Obviously, tidy up the energy research.

Two: Monitor all interdepartmental communication for key words: *Jayna, simulant, Dave, David, Madoc, Constructor*, and half a dozen others.

Three: Create an immediate notification system of any communication between Mayhew McCline and the Constructor.

Four: Investigate the housing riot stats. If anyone did discover her trip to the enclave, some relevant research would provide some plausible cover.

Five: Low priority—mental health indicators among the under-fives. (She hoped Dave was right about the baby but she harbored doubts.)

Six: Finally, and low priority again—continue monitoring the sales at auction houses. There should always be time, she thought, for light relief.

———

The voices of the C6 and C7 residents, now congregating in the canteen, favored the drone of conference delegates rather than the erratic buzz of friends hanging out. All the Franks and Fredas stuck together, thankfully. Jayna couldn't bear making conversation with them; it just didn't work.

"Hello, Jayna." The distinctive singsong voice came from behind her. "We missed you yesterday."

Jayna turned. "Hi, Veronica...and Sunjin." She smiled.

"So where were you?" said Sunjin.

"Events conspired. Backlog of work."

"That's a shame. Sounds a little...chaotic?" said Veronica, frowning.

"Not really. All's fairly normal except...have your meals been changed recently?"

"They have, but only for first sitting," she said. Her friends seemed nonplussed.

"Seeking redress today, Jayna?" Sunjin had beaten her soundly at the last backgammon gathering. Hardly surprising. He was one of the first of their generation. Of all the simulants she'd met, Sunjin was the sharpest. She always sought him out in a crowd.

"I'll not get past you, Sunjin. How are things going anyway? Solved any gruesome crimes lately?"

"I have. And I'm closing in on a couple of murder cases but my prime suspects are already dead." His remit at the Metropolitan Police Department was to examine unsolved cases. He had started with police killings, then child murders and, most recently, he was unearthing some race-hate and sex crimes as well as a string of seemingly unprovoked, random cases of murder. Jayna surmised that his initiation had been all-encompassing: an awesome data handling capacity augmented with keen analytical skills, sociological and psychological know-how, demographics, micro-economics...

"We brought in a serial rapist last week. He's ninety-seven years old; charged him on scientific evidence. But the case won't reach the courts, too senile to stand trial."

"Disappointed?" said Jayna.

"No one seems disappointed at the department. In fact, everyone's celebrating his arrest. Unshakeable attachment to these old cases. Baffles me."

"You'd think they would move forward, find out who's spraying yellow paint on our walls," said Veronica. Jayna and Sunjin nodded in agreement. "I suppose the detectives want to flex their new capabilities. They want to—"

"'Settle old scores.' That's what they say," interrupted Sunjin. "They usually had all the data they needed but they lost track—bad collation, cross-referencing. Tragic all round." Knowing looks were exchanged and Sunjin turned to Jayna: "Do you still have access rights to Police data?"

"For the time being."

"Seen anything interesting? I'm too tied up with old cases to know what's happening on the streets."

"Which streets?"

"I mean, what's happening now."

That policing vernacular, she never saw it coming. "Well, I've seen one or two things. But I'm modeling, looking for correlations rather than root causes." She smiled. "And, I'm certainly not trying to *bring anyone in*. It's all academic."

"Still, you might spot trends that elude the department."

"That's the really fascinating part of our role," said Veronica. "We really can shed new light."

Jayna ignored Veronica. "I suppose I've noticed one matter of potential concern but your people will be well aware of it. In any case, Mayhew McCline will inform the Police of any findings related—"

"Go on," said Sunjin.

"Well, I've noticed five instances of hate crime perpetrated by organics against bionics. I came across it quite by accident. I'm not sure I can make any use of it; could be spurious."

"From what I've seen, hate crimes were traditionally linked with religion"—he counted them out on his fingers—"race and football. But in the case of football it was just an excuse to vent violent tendencies at the end of each working week. Race and religion: those were the issues. But, organics kicking bionics, that's quite another matter. Crime between the economic classes was rarely hate-motivated. Theft on the one hand, exploitation on the other. In general, of course."

———

With two rounds of backgammon completed, Jayna and her friends from C7 congregated by the tea and coffee urns with Sunjin and his friends from C6.

"So, who's still in?" said Veronica. Raised index fingers showed that C7 was holding out well. Sunjin stepped forward, took an institutional cup and saucer, and held down the lever attached to the urn spout. He released a lukewarm surge of coffee-flavored water that swirled and over-topped the cup rim, settling into a murky moat.

"You usually serve plain water." He was irritated.

"Another alteration to the menu, I suppose," said Harry.

"What do you know, Sunjin, about these menu changes? Is there a link to the recalls?" said Julie. "It's something I've been thinking about."

"Recalls? Plural?"

"Yes, we've heard of two recalls. Which one do you know about?"

He hesitated. "A simulant, one of our generation. He went daytripping beyond the city limits without authorization." Jayna's grip on her cup and saucer tightened. "You know about that one?"

Julie responded: "No. We've heard about a simulant at the Liverpool Tax Office who had a curry at a private restaurant. And someone else at the Institute of Forensic Accountancy who was late for meetings. That's all we've—"

"How could it be related to the menu change?" Sunjin barged in.

Julie seemed taken aback. "Well…it was a matter of coincidence, with the curry incident. Very spicy food. Do you see?"

"Maybe." Sunjin seemed to calm himself. "In any case, I'm sure they know what they're doing at the Constructor. A simulant has probably analyzed the situation for them. I think we can trust one of our own." He laughed politely and the others followed suit. Jayna faked a broad smile as best she could and, attempting to extract herself from the discussion, looked down at the tips of her shoes.

"Jayna says the Constructor can't risk any damage to the brand," said Julie.

"I'm sure you're right," he said looking across at Jayna. "The corporate world's your specialist subject."

Their eyes had to meet but she conceded only a glance. Instead she looked around the group. "I think Sunjin knows as much as I do on any subject."

———

In the third round, competing for a place in the semi-finals, Sunjin and Jayna were thrown together. He was playing well but whereas he normally fixed his attention on the board, he now frequently stared into the middle distance. She, too, was making her moves on automatic and found herself imagining Sunjin naked. Was Sunjin capable…? Would he respond…?

"Jayna, do you think these recalled simulants will be sent back to their previous work?"

She shook the dice and made her move. "Depends on the nature of their transgressions. We don't know the full stories."

"If simulants are faulty as a result of the Constructor's error, then they ought to be reinstated and allowed to continue with their work."

"It would be a shame to lose their experience."

"Exactly."

"I think, Sunjin, the pressure would come from the lessee. If Mayhew McCline were getting excellent results from my work, for example, they wouldn't want to risk losing their competitive advantage just because I exhibited a minor glitch, if that were to happen. After all, they contend with mildly disruptive behavior from their organics and bionics."

"So you believe there would be an element of negotiation."

"Most likely."

"I suppose the simulant would have some say in the matter."

"Possibly not. Think about it."

He shook the dice. "You're right. Their evidence would be tainted by the very fact that they had transgressed."

"Yes. It's an interesting conundrum. And…it looks like you've won again."

He was gracious in victory. "Well played."

As they stood to make way for the next duo, Sunjin said, "Let me know if you hear of any more recalls. But don't bother going through Mayhew McCline channels. Just tell me down at the Domes. I don't want anyone misinterpreting the department's interest."

"Okay. Whatever you think."

——

Over dinner that evening they pored over the competition results. C6 had suggested handicapping the event but C7 had politely declined their offer.

"The point is they acknowledged the inherent unfairness," said Lucas. "They're all at least six months older than us."

"The gap is closing though," said Harry.

"Anyway, so much depends on the fall of the dice," said Lucas. "That's why we can't take it too seriously. If we were playing chess, that would be another matter. There would be far more at stake, a true battle of wits."

"Even then, it's not as though we have anything to prove. It's the bionics who become agitated about chess. And they wouldn't stand a chance against any of us," said Harry.

"Not in a month of Sundays," said Lucas.

"Not once in a blue moon," added Julie.

Jayna slipped away from the canteen ahead of her friends just as second-sitting residents gathered at the entrance. Lucas was over-excited about the backgammon results and she couldn't bear any more of his chatter. She pushed through the Franks and Fredas and made her way to the top floor of the rest station. She paused by the *No Access* sign then climbed the two flights of stairs leading up to the roof. While taking off her right shoe, she pushed the emergency door's opening bar and then wedged the shoe between the door and door frame.

The slated main roof was set back from the building's perimeter and Jayna took short, deliberate steps along the access path to an open area at the western end of the building. The strength of the breeze surprised her. She sat down cross-legged and, closing her eyes, she allowed her hair to blow unchecked. It licked and whipped her face but she didn't care. The city hummed and honked below her.

Late afternoon had softened into early evening when a man's voice reached her from below. She knelt up, peered over the parapet, and saw a lorry being reversed into the storage yard opposite the rest station. A man shouted and banged the side of the lorry as the driver maneuvered ridiculously close to the pillared gateway. The iron hinges of the gate scraped along the side of the vehicle.

On the far side of the city, the low spring sun reflected brilliant orange off a single tower block in the suburbs. It must be positioned at the perfect angle to the sun's rays, she thought. Surely, she was one of *many* people seeing this explosion of color. And maybe Dave was checking his beehives. Was he looking across the enclave rooftops at the sunset? She felt warmer towards him now, she realized, but even so…

She imagined an orange fog flowing out from the dazzling tower block. It seeped, slowly, through the streets of the metropolis. And she decided to mimic Dave; she imagined herself flying high. She saw the metropolis now as a low-lying, lumpy scab causing a minor, almost imperceptible, drag on the shifting air masses that crossed farmland and the enclaves, sweeping on and on, across other scabs to other continents.

The orange reflection burned her eyes and she looked down. At the foot of the parapet wall she noticed bits of detritus, leftovers from previous maintenance work, nuggets of congealed tar. How many years had it been lying around? Slowly, she teased out individual pieces from the pile and tossed them one at a time across the street towards the neighboring roof. They didn't all reach.

Evening slipped into night-time. She stood up—no one could see her now. She looked across at the apartment blocks on the opposite side of the shuttle lines. Lights were on in nearly all the apartments and several blinds were open. Lights flickered from consoles. People walked around. Some seemed to be cooking. She imagined that a woman in one apartment was talking through solid walls to a man in the adjacent apartment. Many of them seemed to be alone.

———

Back in her bed, she held the bedclothes tight around her and came to a conclusion. For, in her mind, she'd skimmed a series of flat pebbles that made contact with her memories almost at random. She pinpointed a Saturday afternoon, in week ten, when she'd bought the stick insects on her way to the Repertory Domes. *That's when this journey began,* she told herself. *The ladybirds made me stop—on a screen in the shop window. So perfect. And then I went inside. It wasn't the ladybirds, though, but the stick insects in the next tank that I couldn't resist. They almost weren't there. I had to have them.*

CHAPTER 9

Early mornings at C7 were fine-tuned, as in any home, to minimize the time spent on the aggregation of minor but essential acts of preparation. Nevertheless, Jayna incorporated one unwarranted performance in her own morning rituals, namely, brushing her straight and obedient hair, because it allowed more time for her deodorant to dry. Putting on her blouse, then, became a far more satisfying experience: minimal contact between cloth and damp underarms. So, the full process comprised undressing; wrapping a towel around her torso; washing at her small sink; drying herself; *applying deodorant;* cleaning her teeth; donning underwear, trousers, or skirt; brushing her hair; and, finally, *the blouse.*

What occupied her thoughts as she ambled through this procedure was how she could alter her behavior, further than she had already, without attracting attention. While fastening her shoes, she also wondered if she could make changes to her own person. She ruled out anything that would be noticed at work or at the rest station: cutting her hair, painting her nails, customizing her clothes. Reluctantly, she also ruled out making any discrete skin markings; someone would notice in the showers. So, no home-made tattoos or body painting. Decorating her scalp—now there was a possibility.

As she tended her stick insects, she came to a decision. Marking her body was altogether too reckless. Safer, instead, to carry a secret about her person, conceal something in a pocket or wear something under her standard-issue attire. If discovered it would be easier to explain away.

She knelt alongside her bed and sprayed water through the netted wall of the cage. Then she turned and looked up to the top of the wardrobe. Good idea. She lifted down both the handbook and the small package atop. She scanned the lines of type on the stick insect's paper shroud and with a pen she circled three "m"s, two "e"s, two "o"s, one "n," one "t," one "r" and one "i." She took her jacket from the wardrobe, slipped the shroud into the inside pocket and murmured: "Memento mori."

———

The canteen assistant winked at her but breakfast was otherwise the usual perfunctory weekday affair: porridge, toast, and tea. She ate hastily as she formulated a list of requests for specific backup data on her hydrogen research. She looked around at her friends—no one in conversation. No doubt they were foregrounding their own duties to their licensors. By the time they reached their offices they would be super-crunching at a phenomenal rate; the speed was beyond the grasp of their employers. Remarkable. If their bosses truly appreciated these processing powers they might have reservations. Strange that no one asked how they deployed their spare capacity; they should.

Breakfast over, she rushed her tray to the clearing hatch and, surprising herself, she belched.

With a heavy day ahead, Jayna reverted to her normal short route to the office. As she turned on to Granby Row she noticed a feather dancing along the pavement, a white feather from the underbelly of a pigeon, most likely. It was carried this way and that at the whim of the local air movements—an amalgamation of the prevailing winds with super-impositions from swirling local eddies caused by people and vehicles traversing the now-busy street. By some eerie coincidence, the feather caught a more violent burst of energy and Jayna reached out her hand and caught it at chest height. She felt giggly, scatty. Smiling, she slipped the feather into her breast pocket alongside the paper sarcophagus.

A collection. But a collection of what? A random gathering of ephemera, things that touched her life briefly in some obscure way. She sidestepped two men walking towards her, shoulder-to-shoulder, oblivious, deep in animated exchanges. *Should my collection relate to living things—animals, birds, insects? Difficult to decide when I only have two things. If I really wanted to be a major-league obsessive I know what I'd collect*—she dodged another pedestrian—*I'd collect coffee paraphernalia. And I'd mix odd cups and saucers like...No, I don't want to think about Dave just yet...They could all be white, or off-white, with chips and cracks, which could be fascinating in themselves. I could make still lifes...bring out minor differences in shape and curvature. But maybe I should rely on instinct and chance; it's working well so far.*

One of those awkward commuter moments occurred. Jayna heard clackety heels gaining ground. It was too intimate for strangers to walk side-by-side. Should she slow down, let the woman pass, or maintain her pace...make the woman walk faster? Judging by the rapid approach, she was intent on passing. Over several steps, the woman started to draw alongside but Jayna held her pace. On the verge of losing her conviction, she felt tight grips on both her arms. In seconds she was at the end of an alley, pushed and shoved to the dark back corner behind a black shiny car. She couldn't see who it was, but then: "I want to speak to you." Jayna knew the voice. Yanked around, pushed back, and winded against the brick wall, she gasped, "Ingrid, what—?"

"You've no idea, have you? *Stupid cow.*"

"Please, Ingrid, you're hurting."

"I'm telling you, shut it! I've never been so...*humiliated.*" Her face was hideous. Ingrid tried to shake Jayna but she wasn't big enough. "I had to go home and tell my family. I had to tell them I'd been replaced by a fucking…clone."

Jayna's jaw dropped. "I'm *not* a clone, and it *wasn't* like that." She could smell coconut hair.

Ingrid grabbed Jayna in the crook of her arm and ground her elbow into a brick edge. "Oh? Well, what was it like then, Jayna? Enlighten me, please."

She couldn't bear to look at Ingrid; she spoke to the side wall. "Benjamin took out a contract. I turned up for work. I didn't know you'd be made redundant."

"Well, that's exactly what did happen."

"Ingrid, there wasn't enough work."

She grabbed two handfuls of Jayna's hair and shoved her back against the wall. "You were fucking piling through everything. And I'd had a bad quarter, that's all. Just one bad quarter."

"I'm sorry. But if you hadn't been so mad at Benjamin you'd have got your job back. Tom Blenkinsop—"

"I know about Tom Blenkinsop. What a prize bastard!" She pressed her palms to her temples. "Always taking credit for other people's ideas…*my* ideas." And just as Ingrid turned to retreat she swung back and landed her small fist into Jayna's belly. Low and dirty. She doubled over. Ingrid clutched her wrist. "Christ! Look what you made me do." And she left the alley.

———

Mid-morning, Hester walked over to Jayna and as she opened her mouth to speak she hesitated. "You look pale." But immediately pressed on: "I hear you're on to something. Eloise says you're seeing Benjamin this morning. Well, we always score brownie points for energy intelligence."

Jayna ignored the first remark. "It's taken some ferreting out."

"By fair means or foul?" Jayna attempted a smile but made no reply. "As long as the report stands up. We may need to release it as an Energy Confidential—fewer takers but a much higher fee. Copy me in on progress."

The pain from Ingrid's punch had given way to soreness and a hard ache. Jayna had taken ten minutes in the alleyway to recover. Setting out towards Mayhew McCline, leaving vomit on the polished wheels of the parked car, she'd struggled to keep pace with the other walking commuters. And, entering the cavernous lobby of the Grace Hopper Building for the one-hundred-and-thirty-sixth time, she'd refused the doorman's greeting and ignored Eloise on entering the elevator. As though smoothing the line of her garment, Jayna had slowly brushed her right hand from her left shoulder downwards across the slight stiffness of the paper shroud in her inside breast pocket. That's when she decided. She would not report the incident. *A mugging, for heaven's sake.* There would be so much fuss; they would watch her too closely. And she also decided on a new level of risk-taking:

An Experiment: (As Dave might put it) To fucking show them all.

———

Hester busied around the office all morning, almost hyperactively. Jayna followed her movements. It was so obvious; Hester was excited about the energy report, thinking how to spend her bonus already. Maybe planning a little flutter before the report's release. *I'd do the same if I had the money and I'd make a better job of it than Hester ever could.*

As if trying to conceal her thoughts, she left her array and slipped into the washroom. Locking the end cubicle door, she stared at the gridded tiles lining the external wall and visualized a spreadsheet. She knew Taniyama would disapprove…She stroked a row of tiles above her eye level. If she delayed submitting her draft energy report to Benjamin…until the end of play on Thursday… that would give her four days. First task—with her left forefinger she stroked a column of tiles on the far left—she'd need a series of aliases either invented or hijacked; homework needed on that. Then she'd set up the bank accounts—she ran her finger down the next column of tiles. Raid a few medium-sized corporate deposits— stroking the next column—steering clear of any company with a resident simulant. And she'd make a string of share purchases— stroking another column—all under the false names.

I'll have my investments in place before my draft report is even seen by Benjamin, and well before the final Energy Investment Strategy is released to the outside world.

Hands on hips. A little background research would be handy: bank security reviews, identity fraud, media reports on insider trading together with case notes from the Metropolitan Police Department. No need to re-invent the wheel.

She unlocked the cubicle door, hesitated, and relocked it. She took the spare roll of toilet paper, pushed it as far as she could into the toilet U-bend, flushed, and dashed out.

———

Benjamin, as anticipated, fell into spasms of corporate ecstasy when she reported her hydrogen breakthrough. She requested extended database searches and he pressed for early submission of her draft report: "The sooner this is ready the better. Half-year reviews are coming up and this will look very good for the department."

"And particularly good for you, Benjamin." He beamed. He took the comment at face value; no innuendo, no underpinning of sarcasm, no office politics informing her response. She brought out the best in him. "Good for everyone," he said.

"I'll have the draft ready on Thursday."

"Thursday? You can't make it sooner?"

"I need to find several new sources to replace some that were… intrusively acquired. We may need to brief a friend in the media to ask the right questions of the right people. Then we can quote their comments. But I doubt it will come to that."

As she stood to leave he pointed to her face and made a circle. "You all right? Look a bit peaky."

———

That evening, chatter in the canteen still buzzed around the Sunday social. They trawled through the statistical data from the back-gammon results, looking at individual efforts and seeing which first moves had the best correlation with success and failure. The randomness of the dice throwing was scrutinized, because they could recall every throw. And, they tallied the results according to simulant age and according to their professional work. Everything was exhaustively debated and re-analyzed; the weightings for each variable were fine tuned. Each contributor to the discussion was fully indulged by the group of friends, as they squeezed the maximum satisfaction from what amounted to a communal reminiscence. But Jayna did not contribute.

Sunjin became the subject of conversation and she tuned in.

"Will he always work at the Police Department?" said Lucas.

"Why shouldn't he?" said Harry.

"Well, eventually he'll solve all the old cases. And there can't be many crimes these days."

"Volume isn't the issue. Implantation is increasing the complexity of white-collar crimes, rare as they are. So, I don't think Sunjin will be short of work," said Harry.

"But why would any bionic risk going to prison?" said Lucas, incredulous.

"Faulty screening. Some slip through the net."

Jayna spoke up: "You remember Ingrid? The analyst sacked at Mayhew McCline?" They all nodded. "I think she slipped through the net; problem controlling her temper. Benjamin thinks so, too. Or, at least I think he does. It makes you wonder, doesn't it?...Maybe we should run operations where fraudulent activity is a risk. We wouldn't need much help. We could work quite happily alongside a few well-trained organics." Jayna was now confronted by a vista of bleak expressions. "Just thinking aloud," she said.

"Implantation of organics could be a detour. But I can't imagine today's politicians coming to that conclusion," said Harry. Another round of nodding.

Jayna nudged the conversation further: "It might be commercially driven. Shareholder pressure might be the impetus towards higher employment rates for simulants, might be very attractive to CEOs. And, don't forget, the Constructors are themselves a very powerful sector."

"I can't see it, Jayna," he said firmly.

"No, I agree, Harry. It wouldn't make any sense at all."

It was time for dessert and thus conversation returned to safer ground as they discussed the viscosity of the custard: too thin to stick to the jam sponge. "Really," said Julie, tipping custard off her spoon, "the standard's dropping."

In the recreation time following dinner, Jayna decided she ought to visit Julie in her quarters. She now realized that when she'd last sat on Julie's bed, there had been no uncertainties in her mind; no unexpected, unpredicted events troubling her. They had known nothing, then, of any recalls.

Julie stepped out of her room. "Oh hi, Jayna! We must be psychic. I was just coming to see you."

"It's my turn to come to you."

"So who's counting?"

Jayna smiled at her friend's quip, for she recognized the remark as such, and briefly reveled in their shared propensity for frivolous calculation. "Life is good here in Manchester, isn't it, Julie?" she said. They sat cross-legged on the bed.

"Yes, of course. Why do you say that?"

"Your joke; makes me feel warm. Knowing we're different, like a brotherhood or sisterhood."

"Different and together. You're right. Can you imagine if we didn't live like this? I can't see myself living in an apartment block on my own, not seeing anyone once I closed my front door, eating alone."

"If you had a partner you'd have company."

"I don't know…that kind of exclusivity could be dull. And I can't imagine how I'd choose one person to live with, even a flatmate. I like different things about each of my friends here. You can't roll everything up into one person."

"Physical attraction seems to clinch things for them."

"Even so, they spend a lot of time together when they're not having sex. That's what I think, anyway."

"But if you had to choose someone, Julie, who would it be? You know, just supposing."

"Is this a game?"

"Yes, a silly game."

"Let me see…Sunjin!" They laughed gently and Julie prompted, "Your turn. Who would you choose?"

Difficult. She couldn't mention Dave. "Sunjin would be my first choice, too."

"Really, Jayna, this is a ridiculous game."

"But look what would happen, Julie, if it were true—that we were both attracted to Sunjin. In the born world that could spell trouble. We would hate one another because we were competing for the same man. We'd trample all over our friendship without even thinking about it. You can see how complicated life would be. Sunjin might even encourage us to fight over him. We might end up killing each other." Jayna couldn't stop. "Imagine if you got the man you wanted, and he turned out to be a…cruel and callous person."

Julie looked distressed momentarily. "I see what you mean. I suppose, when you think about it, a lot of song lyrics are about exactly that—jealousy, unfaithfulness, unrequited love. I actually can't think of many happy lyrics."

"Not enough drama, I suppose."

Julie brightened. "I've thought of another game. If you had to sack someone at work, who would it be?"

"Julie, that's terrible. How could you think that?"

"It's only a game, less ridiculous than yours."

"It's more achievable." And, again, the two friends laughed. "I think…no, definitely Hester."

"Because?"

"She doesn't have time for anyone. Well sometimes she does. But she's so impatient. I think she frightens people."

"My turn. I would choose Peterson because he talks endlessly about his family. He can't imagine I'm not interested."

"A very reasonable excuse for dismissal."

"Well, it's a better reason than…" Julie stopped herself.

"What?"

"I'm just thinking about the recalls. It doesn't seem fair."

"Sunjin seemed concerned about them, too. He told me… he didn't like the idea that we wouldn't be consulted, that it was disproportionate."

Julie stood up and started to brush her hair in front of her mirror. "If one of us were recalled and reassigned, would we be stationed somewhere else in the city?"

"More likely, Julie, you'd be reassigned to another part of the country or overseas. You'd have a new name, too, I expect."

"So, a completely new beginning," she said, turning around.

"Most likely. Does that bother you?"

"I don't know. If it made clear sense then it should be easier to accept. I can't help thinking there's a flaw in the argument."

"Well, let's not think about it now. It's not going to happen to you or me."

"I hope not," said Julie, dejected.

"Come on. Let's listen to some music. Lighten up a bit."

Fifteen minutes before lights-out, Jayna took her leave and as she opened the door to her friend's room, Julie said, "Don't let Hester bug you."

CHAPTER 10

Jayna lifted the cage's cover and gingerly rejigged the twigs to create some new angles. The base needed cleaning but she didn't have time. Wretched little things. They would be better off outdoors on some bramble, even bramble on waste ground. She decided to call by the florist. "No reason why you phasmids should suffer just because I'm preoccupied," she murmured. She stood and stamped her right foot into her shoe. They seemed to prefer the variegated ivy. She stamped into her left shoe. A pain pierced through her heel. A small foreign object gouging her skin forced her to stagger backwards. She sat on the edge of her bed, gripped the bedclothes, and ground her heel into her shoe. Her movements were slow and deliberate. Her eyes were brimful.

Crying—an outward sign of sadness in born-humans, preceding any true feeling.

She forced herself to conjure memories—of Dave holding her close, the screaming baby; thoughts already so close to the surface. She stamped her heel again, grinding, more pain and more reflexive tears; an excruciating concoction. The wetness in her eyes swelled, her nasal passages constricted, and she knew that if she blinked the tears would spill. She tipped her head to the right. Thus, the tears overflowed but not down her cheeks. They formed a pool—between her left eye socket and the bridge of her nose—and a small stream that ran from her right eye across her temple and penetrated her hairline. She moved her head to the upright and the small pool emptied; tears ran down into her open, receptive hands. Incoherently, she murmured, "I *will* see him again." The normal measured tones and rhythms of her speech were distorted. She cried silently, spread the tears across her palms, and wiped them down her cheeks.

Recovered, she removed her shoe and turned it over; the foreign object made a tiny but sharp impact on the floor's uncompromising surface. She lifted her left foot onto her knee, began a fingertip search, and found it, the site of a small crater. As she massaged the site, the blood flow increased and the needle of irritation seeped away into the surrounding tissue, spreading the fast-fading pain to the point of complete dissipation. She forced a smile and, with the release from pain, she tasted relief. Salty.

———

"Is Prudence in this morning?" There was no queue at the florist's and Jayna hoped to be in and out quickly.

"No, love. She's in tomorrow."

"Well, Prudence gave me some off-cuts last week for my stick insects and she told me to drop in anytime I needed more. You must be Geena."

"That's right. But it's a bit early for wastage."

"Mid-afternoon?"

"I should have plenty by then. Anything in particular?"

"Rose leaves and ivy would be perfect. Variegated."

Geena looked over Jayna's shoulder at a new customer entering the shop, and smiled.

"Jayna, who are you buying flowers for?" It was Benjamin.

"No!" She shook her head, evidently fazed. "I'm just here for some foliage for my pets."

"Ah! The stick insects. Well, I'm ordering some flowers for my wife. Help me choose some, will you? I never know what to get."

"I usually choose for him," said Geena. "I don't know what he finds so difficult."

"I don't want to choose something she'd hate. She doesn't like lilies. Why would anyone not like lilies?"

"That's obvious. They're funeral flowers," said Geena.

"Not always," he said.

"Puts a lot of people off."

"I'd buy these fuchsia," said Jayna, anxious to speed things up and get away. "They'd be nice on their own."

"That's it then. Decided. I'll collect them at the end of the afternoon. For now, Geena, please make a fuchsia buttonhole for Jayna."

"No, Benjamin, it's not…I've got to go."

"No, you don't. I say so."

As Geena busied herself with the twists and wraps of the buttonhole, Jayna covered her awkwardness by faking an interest in the carnations. Why had Benjamin, she thought, placed her in this difficult position? Everyone would notice the fuchsias. But, then… perhaps, better to be noticed for the flowers than anything else. He stepped forward and pinned the exquisite arrangement to her lapel, the back of his fingers grazing the flat area of her rib cage just below her collarbone. She was aware of inhaling Benjamin's exhaled breath. They left together and, waiting for the elevators, he looked down to her, demanding she return his gaze. She acquiesced, and he smiled.

As the elevator doors opened Jayna came face-to-face with Dave.

His eyes scanned, briefly, intensely, as he tried to read the situation. But before he could make any sense of the flowers, of Benjamin standing a little too close to Jayna, he stepped out, pushed through the crowd, and disappeared.

Soon after starting work, she made an internal call. "Dave, I need some research material archiving later this week. I'll come down now and explain how I want it all organized." Hester noticed Jayna's fast pace across the office but was evidently unfazed, no doubt presuming she was on some sort of mission to complete the energy findings.

————

Dave jumped up. "So, what's with the flowers?"

"Never mind the stupid flowers."

"Did Benjamin give them—?"

"Never mind Benjamin." She jerked her head to the right and stepped behind a pillar, partly obscuring herself from the corridor. "I've decided. I *do* want to see you again. I'll come on Sunday…if that's all right." She pulled Dave close to her as if to whisper in his ear. But she had second thoughts and kissed his upper lip. What was it about his mouth? She pulled herself away, remembering what she'd come for. But she was no longer controlling events. He pulled her back towards him and maneuvered her farther from the door towards the one spot in the room out of sight from the corridor. "I thought we weren't supposed to talk in the office," he said, distracted.

"Everything's changed, Dave. I need to tell you something." She tried to make space between them. "I'm sorting some ideas… there's something you need to do."

"So, you're not here about archiving?" He laughed.

"Yes, I am." She pushed again. "When the Hydrogen Archive reaches the main tower, look for a sub-folder named Sarcophagus. And hide it."

"What?"

"Don't ask, Dave. Just do it."

And, as if he'd completely misunderstood, he walked coolly to the door, closed it, and turned the lock. From that point on, everything seemed to happen at double speed. Looking up at the underside of the shelves, Jayna fleetingly thought of Nicole and the broom cupboard.

———

For the next three days, she worked assiduously and stuffed the Sarcophagus folder with all the data from her covert share dealings. By Thursday afternoon, she had more or less completed the challenge and, unable to stall any further, she submitted her draft report to Benjamin. Before leaving the office she uploaded her archive data to the central storage tower, with the tiny Sarcophagus embedded deep within the material. It contained short and long strings of numerals, no meaningful prose. A few surnames and initials but mostly short sets of capitalized letters. It wouldn't take a code breaker to get the general gist; anyone with finance know-how could make a good guess.

When Dave opened the file, he feigned a bored, slumped posture for the benefit of Craig, who was rummaging around for some ancient management accounts. Dave scanned through the data and wondered if Jayna might be two-thirds mad.

He interred the Sarcophagus in a dark, deep place.

CHAPTER 11

Friday. At the conclusion of a directors' meeting, Jayna's attendance was politely requested at a gathering upstairs; as expected. She knew Olivia would do this—hold a discrete celebration before the final report was even completed. Jayna heard hoots of laughter before opening the boardroom door. High spirits indeed. She found the directors chinking champagne glasses as though the report's revenues were already banked and bonuses already disbursed. Jayna captioned the scene: *Here Today, Somewhere Better Tomorrow.* She wondered if it would occur to any of them to imbibe that very particular cocktail favored in times past (equal measures greed, opportunity, temptation). Fairly unlikely, she thought.

Benjamin basked in Jayna's success, and as he raised his glass, he toasted, "To hydrogen futures."

"So what comes next, Jayna? What are you going to cook up for us?" asked Olivia.

"Oh, I don't know. I think it may be something more mundane." She wanted to cool things down. "The financial implications might be less dramatic."

"No clues for us?"

No harm in spinning something out. "I'm digging around in the economic data for running the enclaves. It may not come to anything but I plan to spend a few more days sifting the data before

I decide if it's worth pursuing. That would be the best time to talk about it." She glanced sideways at *Jesse*.

"But what's your gut feel at the moment?"

"I don't really have a gut feel as such. All I can say is…there's a certain momentum within the data." Many raised eyebrows. She knew that would grab their attention. "It leads me to wonder whether a more interventionist role could be taken in these areas."

"You mean clamping down on spending, on policing," said Benjamin.

"I don't know yet. In fact, the opposite could be true. Higher spending might be the answer. Or at least a more responsive approach."

"But is there a specific problem that needs addressing?" said Olivia. "What can the state offer beyond its current policies? They get a fair minimum wage, subsidized housing, free health care, free transport…What else is there?"

"Nevertheless, Olivia, I've come across data that indicates the authorities are turning a blind eye to dissatisfaction in the enclaves. There are regular riots now when the housing allocations are announced."

"But that's just a local issue for the police," said Benjamin.

"Ideally, though, public policy should not generate unnecessary aggravation. It should be tuned to prevent dissatisfaction from welling up, especially if that anger threatens to spill outside the enclaves."

"Well, it's always good for our image to have an impact on public sector administration," said Olivia. "So if you need any advice come straight to me."

So Jayna decided to venture further. It was easier to suggest something in conversation, almost as an afterthought; better than scheduling an appointment with Olivia because *then* any suggestion she made would appear to be a formal proposal or, more to the point, premeditated. She twisted around to take a sandwich from a platter being offered around the group and as she turned back, she said, "What I may need, Olivia, are some first-hand accounts of the enclaves. Or, ideally, a fact-finding visit."

"What?" said Benjamin. "I don't think so, Jayna. I don't really know the enclaves myself, and how would you—"

"I know the enclaves better than anyone here," Olivia cut in. "I sat on the original Transport Networking Group. Why not visit with one of our own staff who lives in the enclaves? It's perfectly safe if you're with someone who knows the way around. Just keep it low key."

Benjamin quickly changed tack. "You could go with Dave Madoc. He's a dependable sort, doing a pretty good job in Archives."

"What do you think, Olivia? Should I organize something?"

"It's fine by me as long as we have an itinerary on record."

"I could make arrangements for this weekend and assess the situation straight away."

"My guess is you'll drop it. So the sooner you decide the better."

"Could I file for out-of-pocket expenses?"

"Yes. Benjamin, will you sort that out?"

"Sure."

She wanted to rush from the boardroom and tell Dave about the sudden turn of events. Their assignation was now officially sanctioned; no need for secrecy. Her mind chased ahead: suggest to Olivia next week…a long-term investigation…adopt the enclaves as a personal project for the weekends…Dave as an escort. On Monday she would submit a feedback report pointing out that Dave had cancelled his own plans at short notice, that she would need Dave's co-operation for the future…some modest payment… But she didn't chase off to tell him. An audit trail was essential for all their communication. *I'll send him an internal communication straightaway, outlining the proposal, and talk to him face-to-face by mid-afternoon. I'll send the details of my itinerary to Benjamin and*

Olivia, confirm the visit by formal internal communication with Dave and, finally, collect my advance expenses.

————

Leaving Mayhew McCline that afternoon, she slipped into a daydream free-fall: a repeated image of Dave greeting her at the station; a disembodied hand, her own, holding a spoon and stirring vegetables in a wok; repeated glimpses of Dave, naked; better still, Dave reading aloud from one of his books, reading a favorite passage to her with precise emphasis.

On automatic, she crossed at the first junction. Her eyes latched onto a woman walking several steps ahead. Stirred from her blissful musings, she observed the woman's peculiar gait—a lumbering distortion caused by her marginally out-turned feet. This minor peculiarity set her apart from Jayna's world of average-ness, neat-ness, correct-ness. So Jayna, as though adding another object to her collection, walked precisely in the woman's out-turned footsteps. She took the act further. She considered the face that might belong to this woman; surely a slack face, the corners of her mouth definitely turned down, and her eyelids nearly conjoined as though her mind were blinded to anything inessential. The woman could only see the color of the traffic lights and the edge of the pavement. All this Jayna imagined and enacted.

She rocked in her stride and started to embrace her new vacuous persona when she realized that Sunjin was almost upon her. Just a few steps away. She snapped back. He must have seen her. And, indeed, he raised his hand.

"Sunjin! Lost in thought there for a moment. What brings you over here?"

If Sunjin had been bemused by Jayna's pedestrian performance he showed no sign of it. "I want to speak to you. I found an excuse to come to this end of town so I could catch you leaving work." He was clearly preoccupied, single-minded.

"What's happening? What's so important?"

He looked around. "Let's walk back towards C7. Can we take a longer route?"

"Okay. We'll go straight on, take the scenic route…Really, Sunjin, you're being very mysterious."

"Listen up, Jayna." He'd mislaid all the niceties, the small talk. Were these his police mannerisms? "It's Veronica," he said.

The top of her head suddenly felt burning hot. "What about her?"

"She's gone. They took her this morning. The Constructor."

She wanted to lean over the gutter. Her stomach was on the verge of spasm. But she had to smother the impulse. She pushed out the words: "It can't be possible."

"No mistake."

They walked silently and out of step. Her thoughts scrambled ahead. What was Veronica telling them? "Surely, not a recall," she said. "She's so committed to her work, as we all are."

"Seems she was too committed. I've been digging around. That's why I wanted to see you. We must all be very careful."

"What?"

"We must be vigilant."

"What are you talking about?"

"They're not taking any chances. So don't say a wrong word."

"Well, you shouldn't be warning me like this. You know that."

"You can report me if you like. But I suspect you think the same way as I do. Neither of us wants to be reassigned."

"But we have no options, Sunjin. There's nothing to be done about it. And what do you mean, 'she was too committed'?"

"Seems she didn't like her bosses ignoring her advice. Sent a scathing note about managerial incompetence to the chief exec."

They both smiled, though reluctantly, because this was completely believable. It was easy to imagine Veronica's disappointment if she were ignored. Only, her feelings must have turned into something closer to anger. And, of course, they could sympathize with her frustrations—both could write a modest tome about managerial ineptitude. The pavements became congested and they broke off their conversation until they reached the more open area near the central metro stop.

"I still can't take it in…She won't get her old job back, will she?" said Jayna.

"No, of course not."

"It would be different if she were a consultant reporting direct to the chief exec. Once you're inside you have to fit in."

"I think, from now on, we all need to look out for one another, Jayna."

"I'm not sure anyone could have helped Veronica."

"Perhaps not. But maybe if she'd explained her problems to us, she'd have thought twice about a vitriolic attack on her colleagues."

"I see what you mean. But, Sunjin, even discussing our problems could be dangerous. If Veronica had done so she might have been reported by one of us. How do I know you aren't checking on me?"

"I'm not! I'm taking a big risk here. Can't we at least agree, the two of us, to watch each other's back? At least pool our information. Make a few plans."

"Plans! What are you talking about?"

"If they come for us. Or if we think it's imminent."

"We can't plan for anything. It's pointless."

He stopped and turned to her. "The point is this: I'm not letting anyone take me out."

"But you'd have no future without a lease."

"Their loss, not mine. I'd manage."

"Oh! Yes? And where would you live exactly? What would you do for money?"

"I'm in the Police Department. I know how to disappear. I could help you, too."

They turned into Kennedy Street and she felt a wave of claustrophobia. Venetian Gothic windows towered above them and Sunjin shifted closer, shoulder-to-shoulder, and leaned his head towards her. He whispered an address in Enclave W8. "We'd be safe there," he murmured. "For a while."

They fell quiet. Sunjin wanted something in return; she was sure of it. But she held back. *Why am I stealing the money? Surely, in my own mind, I've already decided. I am going to run away. Why else would I be doing it? Just to make a point?* She looked at Sunjin but still didn't speak. *A safe place, I'll need one. I can't expect Dave to help. But Sunjin and I...we could do it. It's the last thing they'd expect—two runaways. And I know precisely what he needs, what he wants from me.* She waited until they neared the end of the quiet backwater. "I know how to raise some funds," she said tentatively. "But it's complicated."

"But you can do it?" he blurted.

"Well, it would be a lot easier with your help: save time. Could you add bio data to some false identities?"

"I can find identities to overwrite or lift complete identities..."

Jayna pursed her lips as though this alone might stem the persistent urge to vomit. They walked a full block without saying a word.

"I have the names already," she said.

"What?"

"There's some cash but it's mainly stocks registered under false names."

"You've already done it?" He laughed. "But why bother with stocks?"

"I like stocks. Anyway, it's a sure thing...So, let's get on with it. Listen up." And she told him the names with perfect recall. He listened intently and kept in perfect step.

"Unbelievable. You're way ahead of me," he said when Jayna had finished. "Leave it to me now. I'll go into HQ over the weekend; mornings are quiet. I'm pretty sure I can work it out."

"Sunjin, you know we can't trust anyone else." But she knew she was stating the obvious and, indeed, he ignored the remark.

"Do you know any more about the recalls?" he asked.

"Yes, I do. The woman at the IFA—Nicole? She was recalled for having sexual contact with another member of staff, an organic as it happens." He turned sharply towards her. "Surprised, Sunjin? I thought you might be. Anyway, I've been doing some research. The recalls are only affecting our generation so obviously it has something to do with our enhancements. The earlier simulants, I reckon, had their olfactory senses stripped down genetically to suppress their libido. But the olfactory stuff has been reinstated, to some degree, in our genetic makeup. Which accounts for the Lamb Biryani in Liverpool." He was transfixed. "You see, Sunjin, the olfactory thing is tied up with emotions and our ability to empathize. The Constructor wants us to melt into the workforce."

"Slow down. I don't really follow."

"Something's gone wrong with this fiddling with the emotions, I think. We're not as compliant as we ought to be. Or at least *some* of us aren't. I think the modification is unstable."

"How did you work all that out?"

"A hunch."

"Have to admit, it sounds plausible. But you might be completely wrong."

"Well, whatever the fundamental reason, the Constructor wasn't expecting all this odd behavior."

They crossed the Rochdale Canal and she knew he'd need to peel off soon.

"By the way, the graffiti sprayers were arrested this morning," he said. "I saw them being taken to the interview rooms."

"And?"

"They're American. Can you believe it? American Rightists."

"But America doesn't have simulants. Why come over here bothering us?"

"Trying to spread the word. Or protect American jobs."

"That sounds more likely. Most corporations have upped sticks."

It was time to split their journeys.

"There *is* something else," Sunjin said. "Julie sent me a fairly strange communication today, at the department. Checking I'm going to the Repertory Domes this weekend. She shouldn't be communicating with me at all."

"That's funny we were chatting the other night...Oh, never mind...I'll try to say something to her, if you like."

"Don't just yet. She'd know we'd been talking."

"Okay. Look, I'll try to see you on Sunday at the Domes, late afternoon. But don't be concerned if I don't make it."

"And I'll get to work on the bio data tomorrow."

"While you're at it, Sunjin, strip out that message from Julie." She sighed heavily. "I can't believe we're talking like this."

"Well, we either take what's coming to us or we don't. What can happen that's worse than a recall? I mean, who the hell do they think they are?"

CHAPTER 12

A **hot southerly wind blew through the city** as she waited at the main C7 entrance for Mayhew McCline's chauffeur. All week she'd assumed she would take the metro to Benjamin's home. At the last minute, however, he booked the company limo to take her the short distance to his inner suburb. This caused a slight perturbation among her friends when Jayna mentioned the change of plan over breakfast; no one expected such privileges. She admitted to herself that corporate life had its upside: canapés in the boardroom, champagne celebrations in the office to toast a new deal, a marriage, a new arrival. Mayhew McCline even had a low-key celebration when Jayna turned up; no champagne but a light buffet with a few words of welcome from Olivia. It seemed they could not stop themselves. Added to that were the day-long brainstormers with senior management, and show-and-tell sessions within her department—showing and telling about favorite films, books, games. And team building. When times were good, corporate bosses were free to splurge time and money. They knew their shareholders all too well; they would refrain from micro-interference as long as the bottom line looked good. It had always been so. Her friends, by contrast, realized that their own paymasters, the English taxpayers, would not countenance such excess within the public sector.

And now, the chauffeur-driven limo. Somehow Jayna's world was a little more charmed than theirs; a suggestion of the exotic, which they could not touch. They all knew that from time to time she would rise above the mundane. But this was not to say they felt envious. It was simply noted, observed. In any case, she would bring home stories to tell over the dinner table. She knew they'd want to know everything about this trip to Benjamin's home. There was a carnivorous and undiscerning interest in all experiences.

She hadn't been sure what to wear to the barbecue so Julie, as if taking part by proxy, had scanned dozens of films for outdoor entertainment scenes. Her favorite was the final scene in an old 2D in which everyone danced to live fiddle music. It was all denim and checkered shirts. Even accounting for the lapse of time since the film's production, Julie advised that over-dressing was a bigger risk than under-dressing.

So, there she stood, wearing a simple, white, sleeveless T-shirt with straight-cut, knee-length shorts and sandals. It was difficult to fine-tune her appearance with her limited accessories. Plain but relaxed and self-consciously empty-handed. Was she supposed to take something with her?

The limo turned into Granby Row. She hoped the chauffeur would drive past the entrance and pull in discreetly at the parking bays just thirty meters down the street. He stopped at the entrance. Perfectly. He walked around to the nearside rear passenger door and opened it wide. She descended the rest station steps, crossed the pavement, and stepped into the vehicle without any deviation from a line perpendicular to the steps. Without doubt, someone in the rest station had witnessed this scene and would recount the incident over lunch. Already, she wished she had never made this plan with Benjamin. She would be wiser to slip along quietly and unnoticed rather than placing herself at the center of other people's conversations.

She took up so little space on the expanse of pale blue leather she felt impelled to say something, anything, to magnify her presence. But she could not be bothered. The chauffeur—she knew his name was John—glanced in his mirror and saw she was looking intently out of her side window. He took the hint and as they journeyed through the city center, together but isolated, the only sounds were a purr from the car's inner workings, a tiny amount of friction noise between the tires and tarmac, and the occasional intrusion of sound-verts triggered by the passing of their vehicle. John evidently found these irritating and eventually he cracked.

"Music?" he offered. She shook her head. The informal vow of silence was lost and, as if his single shattering word now needed company, he started the relationship afresh. "Have you been to Mr. Slater's before? It's a lovely place inside."

"No, I haven't. How long will it take?" She knew the answer but it was an easy line.

"Fifteen minutes at the most. I'll drive past the Prince Will Playing Fields and his house is not far from there. Overlooks—" she tuned out for awhile "—two adjoining semis and had them knocked down, saving part—" tuning out again "—rebuilt behind. Funny though, no one used to like those houses."

"Where do you live, John?" she said, with an effort.

"I have a company grace-and-favor. I'm on twenty-four-hour standby so I'm allocated a small bed-sit in a block near the office."

"Do you like it?"

"Suppose so. It's just a room with a bed. I'd have to give it up if I married. But, the way I see it, I get to drive this car all day and there's no real hassle. And I avoid living in the enclaves." She didn't want to be sucked any further into conversation. She'd done the bare minimum to avoid impoliteness. The fewer people she spoke to, the better. So, she looked out of the window once again.

John took a sharp right from the Southern Expressway formerly known as Princess Parkway. Why, she wondered, would any committee name a road after no particular princess? Why so generic? Why not Patriot Parkway or Royal Parkway? Or, if that were too nationalistic, then why not Democracy Driveway or The People's

Avenue or, if that were too inclusive, why not…? The list could go on. She'd always assumed the metropolitan authorities had re-named the major roads in some sort of efficiency drive; self-explanatory names did make sense. Maybe, from now on, she should resist the obvious or the most convenient explanation. Changing a name, she thought, made the past less easy to visit; names tied people to specific places. Most likely, the name-changes played some role in the Great Relocations to the orbital towns. There was such momentum for radical re-thinking. They must have considered everything. She imagined the one-time coalition ministers weighing up their options. Anything to avoid another major depression; they must have said those very words, or something similar: *Never a fourth!* And it all coincided, fortunately or otherwise, with the lobbying for cognitive implantation. Did they do the right thing, she wondered? Pumping money into a near bottomless pit. A two-generation master plan guaranteeing full employment and cheap labor for every metropolis. Was segregation inevitable, she wondered, or was it the easy option? And at what point, exactly, did the *orbital towns* become known as *enclaves*?

In any case, here was the result, she thought, as the car slowed to a stop: only the likes of Benjamin could afford to live in the inner suburbs. And only the highest earners could afford the pretty villages, haunts for the truly successful.

"Here we are, Miss Jayna." He was out of the car as the final syllable left his mouth, for he was intent on reaching her door before she made any move towards the release. She would prefer to open the door herself but she knew it would be mean-spirited to deny John his finale. This might be the measure of his professionalism: a certain number of steps around the front of the limo, at a certain pace, his body bending awkwardly at each 90-degree turn. It was, she felt, a hurried, ugly movement. She didn't flinch until the door was fully open but she sighed inwardly. She swung both her feet out of the car, and John timed his remark to occur precisely at the moment when she stood fully erect. "Have a lovely afternoon, Miss. I'll collect you in two hours unless I receive other instructions."

At such moments, she felt the lack of a surname. She turned her head through 35 degrees towards John, enough to acknowledge his presence without actually looking him in the face. This was the correct form and one that he would recognize. "Thank you."

As she walked through the front-garden allotment, she assessed Benjamin's home; it was symmetrical, doll-like. John swung the car around in the street. He did so with unnecessary theatricality as though making the point to any onlookers that he was connected to a young woman who was so singular that she deserved only the best of cars and only the best of drivers. How silly, she thought.

Each bay on the double-frontage comprised tall panels of dark glass, jointed in an arc-like arrangement. No trace remained of the original front doors, which presumably had been located side by side so that the hallways lay alongside one another. The two houses were now united by a new entrance lobby—a large glass box that projected into the front garden and maybe penetrated the internal shell of the building. She stiffened at her reflection in the blackened glass; Benjamin's family could be looking at her right now, whereas her gaze could not penetrate the interior life of the house. It was, she felt, a particular type of rudeness; an architectural discourtesy. She listened hard in the hope of hearing some unrehearsed, care-free talk on the other side, of hearing family members at ease with one another, so familiar that their actions were instinctive, knowing how to make one another smile, knowing how far they could push. Reluctantly, she took a short step forward, realizing that the family within would alter themselves as soon as they knew of her presence.

The doorbell should have triggered by now, she thought. And, in that moment, she sensed that inner sliding doors were opening, allowing a fuggy brighter light to reach her from either the interior lighting or from a garden beyond. Moving matter, the familiar shape of Benjamin, partially blocked this light.

"Hey, Jayna. You're the first to arrive. That's great. We can have a chat and you can meet the family before it gets busy."

"Who else is coming, Benjamin?" She was startled; she'd failed to anticipate this possibility. Why hadn't he told her other people were involved? He'd given her no indication that she'd meet anyone other than his wife and daughter.

"Just a few neighbors and their children. No point lighting the barbecue if we don't fill it."

"I suppose not." But she was thrown. Benjamin had misled her. Did his wife take charge of the arrangements? She heard voices coming from the back of the house, and when Benjamin's wife and daughter arrived in the hallway, laughing—the young girl half walking, half sliding over the wooden floor—Jayna glimpsed an intimacy, just momentarily, that they now surrendered. It was a subtle adjustment. The incised laughter wrinkles on his wife's face faded to leave a gentler expression that still disarmed her. Any annoyance with Benjamin evaporated.

"Meet Evelyn, and our daughter Alice."

"I've heard such a lot about you, Jayna," said Evelyn. But the introductions were interrupted by scuffling noises as five White Terriers slid into the hallway, falling over one another. Alice shrieked with laughter.

"Switch them off, Alice," said Benjamin. She grimaced and her shoulders slumped. "House Rules. Not when we have visitors." She knelt down and the dogs jumped around her. "Go to sleep," she said to them. And they vanished.

Evelyn guided Jayna with a gentle touch towards open double doors and the rear of the house. An aesthetic of rigid simplicity pervaded the interior, a style she recognized from advertisements. Here was simplicity in its idealized form; the polar opposite of her own quarters with its pared-back utility. It felt like a walk through a dream, for the hallway was virtually bare; so little for her eyes to fix on. She was only aware of the geometry of the space and the character of the finishes, and the way the falling light revealed the different reflectivity of the cream and white surfaces. She suspected the subtlety of the color scheme was far from accidental, that some historical reference had been carefully considered and adapted. The original interior must have been ripped out long ago and it was difficult to imagine how it might have been. Still, it would be interesting to understand how Benjamin and Evelyn had created this home from a knowledge of past mores and their own personal tastes.

"Come through and I'll fix you a drink. Benjamin needs to tidy the garden canopies and I'm just finishing the salads. Come and sit with me."

Jayna had to reconfigure; her boss fixing things, doing chores. She stretched to sit on a bar stool by the kitchen worktop and, while Evelyn prepared drinks, she watched Benjamin move along the garden, turning the handles that tautened the overhead black gauzes. Alice insisted on helping her father and Jayna could see the job would be completed sooner if he were left alone. "Alice seems to like helping," said Jayna.

Evelyn pushed a drink towards her—lead cut crystal, sparkling water, slices of lime. "She's always under our feet like that. She's a very practical little girl, wants to be involved in everything. That's why this salad isn't finished. She wanted to help with the chopping."

"I thought Alice would be playing with toys."

"She's one of those children who skips the whole toy thing."

"But I thought all children played with toys."

"Well, not Alice. Not much anyway. She's happier with a ball of string."

"What would she do with it?"

"Tie the whole house up." Evelyn laughed. "She's done that before."

"I don't really know much about children. I've only met Jon-Jo, Hester's son."

"I don't expect you have much opportunity," said Evelyn, adding after a pause, "You probably don't realize it, Jayna, but you're making a big difference to our family life. We're seeing a lot more of Benjamin and he's like his old self, when I first met him. A lot more relaxed."

"That's good to hear. It would be a shame to miss out on family life."

"We could do with someone like you where I work."

"Where's that, Evelyn?"

"In town, at a law practice. But we're not big enough yet to afford…your skills."

Jayna smiled. Evelyn could have referred to leases. Time to change the conversation. "Does your salad have a name?" Which to Evelyn seemed a comical way of phrasing the question, as though Jayna were asking about a family pet. A broad smile kept a rising giggle at bay. "It's a Mediterranean Salad."

"I guess that's a misnomer?"

"Quite right. The ingredients are all from the garden…Why don't you mix the dressing for me?" And she pushed across a collection of bottles, salt and pepper mills, and an empty jar.

Jayna raised her eyebrows and smiled. "I don't cook, you know."

"Well, it hardly counts as cooking. You're just throwing a few things together. To be honest, that's the best kind of cooking in my book. Good ingredients, lots of chopping." Jayna lifted a jar of English mustard. What should she do with this? "Just mix a few things together in the jar and shake; more vinegar than oil. Then dip a piece of lettuce to test it. Decide yourself."

"Sounds easy enough." She began opening the bottles and poured the oil. A drop more, another drop, maybe another. And the vinegar? How much in proportion to the oil? She was a chemist titrating—too much and she would overshoot the endpoint.

"Go on," Evelyn gently encouraged, "now the salt and pepper, herbs…" Jayna ground black peppercorns into the mixing jar and the grinding sounds took her thoughts straight to Dave and her perfect cup of coffee. What was he doing right now? A single grinding of salt. Mixed herbs, probably too many. She swilled the contents in the jar.

"Put the lid on and shake it hard."

"Okay. But, oil is immiscible. It's going to separate out."

"We put the dressing in a dish with a tiny whisk. See?" She pointed to a shelf of kitchen apparatus, all perfectly aligned and coordinated. "Just shake the bottle." Which she did. "You're learning fast, Jayna."

"I need to. Your guests will be here soon."

At which point Benjamin walked back along the garden and into the kitchen. "I think Alice and her friends have been playing games with the canopies. There's all sorts of junk up there." And, sure enough, they looked out into the garden and saw Alice throwing twigs as high as she could into the air.

"It must be lovely and cool under there," said Jayna.

"We couldn't manage without it. We can use the garden most of the year."

"Well, I must say, your whole home is lovely."

Benjamin smiled and turned to his wife. The smile spread to Evelyn just as Alice hurtled in from the garden and threw herself at her parents for no apparent reason, arms around both their waists. "I love parties. When's everyone arriving? *They're…all…late.*"

They laughed at their daughter's impatience. Eye contact flicked among the three of them, from mother to child, child to mother, child to father. An adult hand placed on a small shoulder, and a stroke of her hair. Alice leaned her head into her mother's stomach, then looked up and raised her hand awkwardly towards her mother's face. "I just can't wait any longer."

How could actors ever replicate such a scene, wondered Jayna? The adulation in these parents' eyes couldn't be matched. Benjamin now picked up the child and kissed her. "It's just as well they're late with all the mess I've had to clear away in the garden."

"Don't be boring, Dad…Put me down."

Such a special child, Jayna thought. But in that instant, as the thought streamed through her mind, she realized that Alice could have been a different child. She might never have existed; a boy child could be here in this room if Benjamin and Evelyn had conceived the child a few minutes later, or earlier. And Jayna couldn't stop herself imagining these two adults between sheets. Maybe they knew that Alice was just one expression of their genes, that many more children were not realized. Maybe every parent knew this.

She imagined the room full of Alice's unrealized siblings and looked for similarities, trying to read character traits in their faces. She noticed, too, those children who stood out, being markedly different, possible throwbacks to long-forgotten ancestors. How would you choose, if you had to? She could almost touch a sense of incredulity on the part of Benjamin and Evelyn that they had produced even one such wonderful creature. She watched Alice gently squirm out of her father's arms. Was their happiness tempered by fear, she wondered? A pearl could be lost more easily than found through happenstance, through carelessness. How did they cope with such vulnerability?

Jayna could feel her heart pumping. She had never witnessed anything remotely similar to this scene—the child's enthusiasm, her parents' delight, simple and untainted. She had never before in her brief life shared a room with such happiness. The inhabitants seemed to merge with the pureness of the space. She returned to her vinaigrette, her eyes misting. "I think it might be too oily."

"Here, add a slosh of red wine," said Evelyn. Jayna duly tipped the bottle, slowly, as she assessed a *slosh*. And she watched the nervous articulation of her arm movement, seeing the contradictory relaxation and contraction of her musculature as she dithered. These movements were made without any need to consciously direct each and every tendon and muscle. In much the same way, each of her thoughts passed through her mind spontaneously, unedited. Only, whereas the muscle movements were indicated in the changing contours of her skin, her inner thoughts lay unrevealed. She was smooth on the surface.

"What do you think, Evelyn?"

With a flourish, Evelyn dunked a strip of lettuce. "Perfect. Simply perfect. See, there's no mystery," she said, and wiped drips from her chin.

Benjamin and Alice returned to the garden to heat the barbecue. Jayna would have followed but Evelyn caught her attention by tapping the point of her knife against the chopping board. "Listen, do you mind if I ask you something…before everyone arrives? I debated this with Benjamin last night and he feels he shouldn't ask, that it's crossing the line." She resumed chopping. "You know, we were talking…because of your visit today." Evelyn bit the corner of her mouth but Jayna couldn't tell if this was related to the vegetable chopping or the approaching question. Evelyn pressed on. "I know you didn't have a childhood as such, that you just woke up fully…" It wasn't the chopping.

"Some say we're *cultured* or *cultivated*."

There was an uncomfortable slippage of meaning with each of these words and Evelyn seemed to stall. "Yes…well, what can I say? Benjamin just raves about the work you're doing. You must get a lot of praise, but do you feel that you've missed out? Am I being rude? What I really mean is, you know, when you don't have parents… We were talking about Alice and how we can trace some of her little ways back to one of us, or even to an aunt or grandparent. I'm sorry, do you mind me asking?" Her face crumpled; embarrassed by her own questions.

"No, Evelyn. It's fine. No one has asked me before, but then some people seem to lack curiosity."

"Afraid of being discourteous…I'm just puzzled, as a parent, and I suppose being a lawyer…wonder where the boundaries are."

"Don't forget, there are born-humans who don't live with their biological parents. Just like them, I don't know my origins. The

main difference for me is that my genetic make-up is derived from
so many sources that I probably have hundreds of parents. You see,
Evelyn, the master-type is the closest I have to a parent. My master-
type would be someone with analytical prowess. That base coding is
then heavily modified. But I don't know if my specific master-type
was a man or a woman. Basically, it would be impossible for anyone
like me to be born from just two parents. What you and I have in
common is our implants but the fact is that I can make better use
of mine."

"It's just—"

She had to cut this short. "It's a fascinating question for lawyers,
I'm sure. But it's not an issue for me."

"Really. I can't imagine…"

The doorbell sounded and Alice raced through from the garden, ahead of her father, repeating her slip-slide performance.

"She's adorable," said Jayna. Evelyn looked quizzically at her.
"Do your visitors know who I am?" This could be her last chance to
speak to Evelyn alone.

"Don't worry. They just know you're one of Benjamin's colleagues. We thought it would be unfair to make you the center of
attention."

"You're right. That wasn't the point of this at all."

"We can always tell them afterwards."

"I'm still a novelty, aren't I?"

"To be honest, you are. And you're welcome all the same." For
Evelyn could turn on the charm, too.

A gaggle came through into the kitchen; at least four people
talking simultaneously and all throwing their voices as though their
audience congregated at the far end of the garden. It seemed the
women's voices became higher pitched as the men's voices boomed
lower and lower. Three children ran with Alice across the kitchen
and into the garden, quickly followed by two more, at such speed
that Jayna assumed they already had an agreed game plan for the

afternoon. Any delay could only result in pleasures lost. Evelyn walked around the kitchen work area and slipped into kissing rituals with the guests. And both Benjamin and Evelyn accepted bottles of wine and small gifts.

Her previous intimacy with Evelyn had come to an abrupt end and she found herself on the periphery of several parallel conversations apparently centered on people not present—older children living away from home, friends who couldn't make it today. Others then splintered into separate recountings of recent holidays—how they'd traveled, when they'd returned home. Meanwhile, drinks were being organized and people called out their choices. And in the middle of this stood Benjamin. Sitting a little way from the group, she reassessed her boss. At work he was vigilant, keeping close tabs on everyone's projects, always pushing them along, clearing obstacles, eager to invoice, and constantly mindful that hard work should translate into strong profits. More than once, she'd heard him say: "Any fool can keep busy." But *here* he was convivial, affable, throwing an arm around his friend's shoulder, exchanging affectionate double kisses with the women. The private life of Benjamin Slater, she thought. It was all so physical. She also reassessed the incident last week when he touched her arm. Maybe his office persona slipped momentarily.

"And, everyone," Evelyn raised her voice, "meet Jayna from Benjamin's office." Jayna met everyone's smiles and salutations with a broad smile of her own and raised her glass to shoulder-height, that is, not too demonstrably. Evelyn waved her over and a round of hand-shaking started—the entire group realizing this to be the correct form (a) for someone they were meeting for the first time, (b) for a friend's colleague, and (c) for a young adult.

"Come on then, Jayna, give us the dirt. What's he like as a boss?" asked a women with short cropped hair.

"Maybe she's my boss," responded Benjamin.

"Well, I'm not," she said, wondering if she should relax and sound a little more regular.

"So, what's he like?" the woman persisted.

She smiled and lifted her chin. "Actually, he hardly does a stroke of work all day."

"Just as I suspected," said Evelyn.

"Totally believable. Lazy bastard. I bet you do all his work," said the woman.

"It feels like it sometimes," she pushed.

"Truth's out, Benjamin," said Evelyn.

"It just goes to show what a nice guy I really am when a member of staff can have a go at me, and—" turning to his underling "—by the way, you're fired." As the group of friends chortled at Benjamin's remark, the doorbell rang and Jayna used the interruption to begin a subtle but purposeful disengagement. For her main interest lay elsewhere. More than anything else, she was desperate to know exactly what the children were doing in the garden. The opportunity came as the new arrivals entered the room, as faces turned to meet and match one another's expressions of expectation and…happiness (yes, it was definitely happiness that Benjamin and Evelyn's guests were sharing). She stepped onto the patio and edged with trepidation nearer the little people. They were self-absorbed to the point of implosion, so there was little danger that her approach would arrest their activities. However, she was surprised by the relative peace. They were barely communicating with one another as they darted back and forth to the edges of the garden, performing what seemed to be pre-determined missions, searching, collecting; each in the midst of some half-crazed personal quest. The adults and their offspring were clearly in separate orbits.

She moved still closer and feigned an interest in a climbing plant halfway between the patio and the center of the children's activities. A boy grabbed a handful of pebbles from the plant pot by her feet, leaving the soil exposed to the sunlight that screamed through the gap between the gauze shades and the boundary fence. He placed the pebbles one at a time on the ground to demarcate a circle, which matched two other circles on the garden large enough to allow two children to kneel within their perimeters.

Jayna caught Alice's eye. "What are the circles for?"

"They're trading posts but we're not ready to start yet," and off she went to the shrubbery at the bottom of the garden.

What sort of make-believe could this be? And why were they playing with such urgency? Was it the kind of game where most of the effort went into preparation, the game's execution being instantaneous? Like a game of chess with 99 per cent of the game comprising thinking time and barely one per cent spent moving the pieces. Or, like a competition when the outcome was based on a momentary judgment. But maybe, Jayna thought, there was another factor that drove the children to these levels of mania. Time itself might be the issue; a factor beyond the children's control. No doubt, if the adults chose to, they could bring an abrupt end to these highly charged activities. The supposed freedom of the children was, she decided, more an illusion than a reality.

Alice returned to her circle with two small feathers and several flower heads. She looked up at Jayna. "It's okay. We're allowed to pick the weeds. Mum and Dad leave them for us." She laid the flowers side by side and added the feathers as soft parentheses at each end of the line. She took a twig from a small pile she'd accumulated and began scraping off the bark vigorously with her nail to reveal the smooth whiteness of the naked form beneath. Jayna placed her hand around the paper sarcophagus in her shorts' pocket and her body shuddered involuntarily. *We're playing the same game.* But Alice, it was clear to Jayna, had the keen eye of a creature who lived closer to nature; someone who would sprawl out on the ground and rub her index finger on the bare compacted earth between individual blades of grass. She was bound to find interesting things.

"Why the big rush?" she asked Alice.

"When the grown-ups come out we won't have much room. But I've made Mum promise to keep everyone near the patio." And off she ran again.

The rest of the children might have been oblivious, initially, to Jayna's presence but from their occasional glances in her direction and their exaggerated efforts it seemed they were now trying to impress her, evidently pleased that an adult should want to see what they were doing instead of chatting with their parents indoors. But, of course, she wasn't as old as their parents and her clothes were like play-clothes.

"Do you want to be the umpire?" asked Alice.

"I don't know the rules."

"Well, if we can't agree on a trade you have to decide. And, you have to stop any team stealing from two trading posts at the same time. And, you can't take your things with you on a raid. You have to leave it all in your circle."

"Raids? Can you go on a raid any time you like?"

"No, only when you're running very low, like if you've done a big trade of a lot of your things for one special thing like a feather."

"Okay then. But you'll have to tell me if I'm getting it wrong. Tell me when you've started the game."

And so it happened that ten minutes later when Alice decided—this being her garden and therefore she made the big decisions—that trading could begin, Jayna was called on to judge the trade of two all-white pebbles for a stripped twig. "I think the twig took a lot of work so I think you need to offer more than two nice pebbles."

No arguments. Her word was taken as the law. Then came the raid. While two of the children were embroiled in a trade, Alice and her team-mate hurled themselves towards a vacated circle to loot their goods. Instantly, the negotiators broke away. Everyone dived to defend their circles and one boy reached Alice's circle before she could return. He grabbed one of her precious feathers. Despite the

aggressiveness of these movements, there were no wild cries of com-
plaint or indignation. Doleful sighs came from the losers and the
children made a quiet examination of the net losses and gains.

"Well, was it worth it?" said Jayna.

"Not really. Not this time. But I did get this lovely dead wasp
and it's hardly damaged."

"Just dead!"

"I'm going to put it on this red leaf so it looks like it's having a
little nap."

Jayna gazed around the small group of children fixed in their
fantasy world of inanimate and deadly treasures. The rules of the
game were shockingly free of any moral base. Stealing was condoned. There were no repercussions. No one was sent to a make-
believe jail. Yet in stark contrast, the participants would calmly
negotiate the relative values of a flower head, a particularly straight
twig, an interesting piece of stone. These values had probably been
determined over several games so that all the children had a feel for
how the currency worked. Did they think the world operated like
this? Was this their attempt to emulate the adult arena in which
some people did well and others did not?

Benjamin was already preparing the barbecue and his friends
spilled out onto the patio. Evelyn called: "Now don't interrupt the
kids' game. Give them space." Jayna doubted the adults registered
the appeal. She walked back towards the house, casting looks over
her shoulder towards the children.

"Steak and salad okay for you, Jayna?" asked Benjamin.

"Perfect," she said. "Let me help."

CHAPTER 13

"**We went to the University Park** this afternoon on your recommendation, Jayna," said Lucas as she joined them at dinner. Truth was, she'd never stepped foot in the park, only seen it through the railings. It was an alibi she'd fabricated for her assignation last weekend with Dave. She'd described, at some length, a lazy afternoon spent lying around on the grass. Would the story come back to bite her?

"We're all completely baffled," he said. "There was a really strange altercation between the ice-cream vendor and one of his customers. She bought a choc-ice and complained that the chocolate tasted burnt."

"Can you burn chocolate?" said Jayna.

"Well, the ice-cream man said the choc-ices were a specialty, home-made. He called them Black Menorcas and said they were an 'acquired taste.'"

"Black Menorcas?" said Jayna.

"I did some research when I got back and it turns out that Black Menorcas are a breed of *chicken*," he said, bemused, "originating in Spain. I don't understand."

"Maybe it's a personal issue. His family might keep chickens or did so in the past," said Jayna. "Even so, I don't see why anyone would name a choc-ice after a chicken."

"Logic doesn't always come into it," said Harry.

"Well, I'm going back next week and I'm going to ask him," said Lucas.

With the Black Menorcas dealt with, Jayna became the focus of attention. An interrogation began on her visit to Benjamin's.

"So what was the biggest eye-opener?" said Julie.

"I hadn't realized that Benjamin would invite half the street." She didn't mean exactly half the street but she'd heard the phrase at work and was fascinated by the use of *half* the street rather than the *whole* street, as though *half* the street paradoxically carried greater emphasis, or was somehow funny. "Rather, I'd imagined the four of us would sit on big sofas in a formal reception room—have a quiet chat before they started the barbecue. But, as it turned out, it was all extremely informal. I chatted in the kitchen with Benjamin's wife, Evelyn, while we made the salads and dressing."

"Making salads? You, Jayna?" said Julie.

"Evelyn told me what to do. And later, I helped turn the meat on the barbecue."

Julie leaned forward. She clearly wanted the details so Jayna obliged. "You have to cook steak at extremely high temperatures. The art is knowing when to remove the meat. A minute too long and it will be too dry." The group was now fully attentive. "Some guests wanted their steak rare so the secret is to take the meat off sooner than you think; that way if it's too rare the guest can put the meat back on the barbecue for a couple more minutes."

"And was it fun?" asked Lucas.

"I suppose it was. But it all seemed so much effort for Benjamin and Evelyn: preparing the food, the cooking, serving the guests, clearing up. In fact, the whole event revolved around food. Everyone talked in great detail about the salads—which crops were doing well on the allotment, which were disappointing this season—the availability of specific ingredients, the cut of the meats. I'd no idea it would be such a big issue."

"We just go to the canteen, eat whatever is served, and walk away," said Lucas.

"Seems a lot of work," said Harry, unimpressed.

"Well, their guests did help now and then. One person started to collect dirty plates and others followed suit. One of the men helped to serve drinks. And everyone helped to organize the children— they ate first, but on less expensive cuts of meat."

"Why?" asked Lucas, wide-eyed.

"I really don't know. I didn't like to ask. To me, it seemed a double economy because the children ate less anyway." While on the subject of the children, she described their game playing.

"The basis of the game might go back a long way," said Harry. "Maybe there are older, similar games that act as templates, that they repeat and slightly adjust."

"Children like activities based on swapping things. And running around is another big thing," said Julie helpfully.

"But what about the stealing? That's what I can't understand," said Jayna.

"If they only steal in a crisis, that's not so bad. It's painfully realistic…if you watch the news. That's down to natural instinct," said Harry.

Natural instinct. She was sure she was blushing. And now she recalled another instinct; she'd felt jealous of little Alice Slater. That particular feeling had erupted when Jayna left the Slater home. She'd said goodbye to Benjamin and Evelyn and, as she walked towards the limo, Alice had charged out of the house shouting, "Take this! The umpire always gets a prize." She handed her a stripped twig. "It's my best one." Jayna had stared down at what was, by then, a slightly grubby artifact and said, "Tell me something, Alice, is there anything that still makes you cry?" Alice took her hand as though they were the same age and were about to skip down the street together. "When my friends are nasty to me, I come home crying and my mum says that's just the way little girls *are* and they'll all grow out of it. But if it gets really bad she speaks to their mums and to my teacher. Then teacher has a chat with us all and makes us all say we're sorry and we shake hands. Then we're best friends again."

Jayna had then stroked Alice's hair and ventured another question: "Do you know what you want to be when you grow up?"

It was Alice's reply to this second question that made her jealous: "I'm only *eight* years old."

So, Alice was a much-loved child, free to play games with no concerns for the future. Jayna, though, surmised a wider narrative. This young girl was unaware that her parents were already watching for the tiniest signs of her natural talents, which they would nurture. And they would assist Alice in realizing her talents as she entered adult life so that, over the subsequent years, the rewards of professional success would fall into her lap as naturally as a fallen branch followed a watercourse to the open seas. She would enjoy some equivalent of her parents' lovely white and cream home. There would be crisp Mediterranean salads, medium rare steaks, fine wine, and fresh ground coffee. Jayna recalled one of Hester's sayings, quite puerile now that she considered it: *What you've never had, you'll never miss.*

Lucas and Harry were stacking the pudding dishes noisily.

"Jayna, you will come out with us tomorrow, won't you? It's the karaoke semis," said Julie.

"I'll join you later in the afternoon. I have a new assignment for the day."

"On a Sunday?" said Harry.

She could be upfront now. "Olivia wants me to do some research on the enclaves so they've arranged for me to visit a member of staff who lives in Enclave W3."

"An enclave? Do you really need to go there? You must have all the reports you need," said Julie.

"They want me to see it for myself. The reports might be missing something or I might be misinterpreting them. I'll be escorted around the area for a few hours; should be back sometime around mid-afternoon."

"But why on a Sunday?"

"It's all very speculative. Nothing may come of it so I volunteered to make the visit outside office hours."

"You don't have to do that," said Julie, almost indignant.

"It's give and take, really. I did have an interesting time at Benjamin's today. He didn't have to invite me."

"I suppose not."

Harry chipped in: "I think I should arrange a trip to the enclaves. If it makes sense for you to go there, it makes even more sense for me to take a look. We have a great deal to say on enclave policies."

Jayna wondered if he had any idea how those policies affected the likes of Dave.

"I'll be interested to hear how you get on," Harry added.

And, as usual for a Saturday evening, they regrouped, taking their drab coffee to their drab common room. On this particular evening, they passed easy conversation about karaoke and Jayna could relax because Julie was always the driver for this topic. Not only did she know the statistics for the most frequently performed karaoke songs but she had also studied their success rates. From the competition results in the UK's major entertainment zones, Julie could give the statistical chances of success for different songs, depending on the sex of the performer and region of the country. (Some accents just didn't work with certain songs, Julie had said.) She knew the chances of a less popular song winning to be less than 20 per cent. She worked with the results of quarter- and semifinalists on the assumption that the tone-deaf and luck-luster competitors had been weeded out by that stage.

"Julie, why don't you enter…see how far you can get?" said Lucas. "You're pretty good."

"I don't think it's a good idea."

"Why not?" he said.

"Maybe it wouldn't be fair."

"I don't see why. It's not as though you were intended to have a great voice."

"I guess not. I expect it's just an accident."

"I don't think you can call perfect pitch an accident," said Jayna. "You make it sound as though it's a problem."

"Well, we all know we wouldn't enter quizzes of any kind. I mean, I'm perfectly comfortable competing with other rest stations but it's different at the Domes. We can always work out how to do something better than everyone else…Anyway, what would be the point in winning?"

Which brought that particular conversation to a dead end.

———

On the roof again with one shoe on, one shoe off. Over the past week, she'd grabbed every chance to steal away after dinner. It didn't always work out. She told herself she wanted time alone but if she were honest she'd admit she wanted to watch the apartment block opposite. She spent hours following the movements of people within their private spaces. Straining to hear any arguments, looking for real families. But this was an inner-city apartment block and that meant well-paid singletons living alone or sharing. And, tonight, she recognized they all had the same easy movement that she'd noticed at the Slaters'—the way Evelyn negotiated her way around her home, the way she knew the contents of every kitchen cupboard (and the way Alice knew every weed at the bottom of the garden). She noticed how each resident could walk from one room to another, from the kitchen to the living area, to the bedroom, to the bathroom, without walking through a communal corridor. Not like the rest station at all. They had multiple personal spaces, not to mention private balconies with the ubiquitous potted fig trees.

It was a hot night. Sliding doors were open in the apartment block and fly screens were drawn closed. *Is it inevitable now?* She slapped a mosquito dead on her knee. *I'm on a path and it's leading me towards a gaping hole; I'm bound to fall in. But, perhaps I should see it differently. I'm on a path that leads to a mountain, or an escarpment. I'm not heading for a downfall. I'm* climbing…*away from all the rules and restrictions. I can see it. I'm sitting cross-legged on a grassy ledge high up on the mountainside. It's dewy and fresh and I'm looking down on everything I've left behind.*

She watched two figures leave a balcony. They entered their bedroom, switched on the lights. The lights then dimmed. One of the figures approached the window and shut the blinds.

She didn't care about the dangers. An ambulance siren screamed somewhere close by. She crept back to the roof access, retrieved her shoe, and took from her pocket a cheap metal teaspoon that she'd taken from the canteen four days earlier. She held the bowl of the spoon, with her thumb close to the tip, and scraped it hard along the wall as she walked down the stairs. With every three steps, she paused and made a small gouge in the wall. Small flakes of paint and plaster dust dropped to the steps. Whenever she found an old blemish on the wall she worked into it, grinding and enlarging the hole to make a much larger fissure. So satisfying. Her vandalism was carefully measured and was partly disguised because the cream paintwork was similar in tone to the gray plasterwork underneath. This encouraged her to do more. She made her marks at different heights. With a high scratch she saw a wardrobe catching the wall. With a low gouge she saw a chair carelessly man-handled. The scratches at thigh height were the buckles on bags.

Three flights down she sat on a step, leaned against the wall, and looked up at the stairwell. The dimmed lights still picked out the scars. If only she could add color. Some minutes later she stood and spread her hands across the wall, feeling the marks with her palms and fingertips. She laid her cheek against the cool surface.

——

Her room lights had already faded. She let her clothes drop to the floor and crawled into bed naked. She tried to slide into the shallows of sleep but the tap at her sink had developed a drip, at four-second intervals.

CHAPTER 14

Toast, scrambled eggs, sausage, and orange juice. Sunday breakfast was her favorite meal of the week. The canteen assistant piled her plate and looked up. "Extra egg?"

"No thanks."

He withheld the plate. "It's not a proper fry-up, y'know."

"Excuse me?"

"It should 'av' bacon, black puddin', and fried bread as well. But they said it's too un'ealthy"—he passed the plate to her—"an' bacon's way too pricey."

"I'm not sure I could eat so much in one meal."

"Yer've not lived till yer've 'ad a proper fry-up."

"I expect not."

She had arrived early for breakfast and now sat alone. Resting her elbows on the table she massaged the muscles at the back of her neck. Avoiding her friends; the half-truths were making her tense. But what else could she do? She positioned the components of her meal as though banishing uncertainty: a two-centimeter gap between her plate and her knife to the right, fork to the left; her glass, four centimeters from the tip of her knife, with the center point of the glass base sited on the axis of the knife; bread plate positioned to the left of her fork, centers of both plates aligned. And then, she could begin. First, she buttered the toast using three sweeps of her knife, inserting the knife inside the soft interior of the bread to clear the metal surface.

She'd heard people talk of the holy trinity of food (bread, cheese, and red wine, apparently) but for her there was no better combination than hot buttered toast and room-temperature orange juice. They were made for one another. She indulged in this private reverie while thinking, thinking very hard. What to do about Dave? She tapped the tip of her knife on the table. *I definitely need to sort something out.*

———

There had to be at least one overlooked treasure, she thought, as she pushed open the door of the antiques shop.

"Hello. Need any help?" A slight woman wearing red, dark hair scraped back.

"I'm looking for a small birthday gift." Excellent. No resident Freda; too small an enterprise. Something was bound to be undervalued. That's how it worked. Antiques shifted from one source to another, from jumble stalls to junk shops, to general antiques dealers, to specialist dealers, and then the auction houses. Just like a food chain: everything progressively consumed by bigger and bigger beasts with larger appetites and tighter niches. But anyone with know-how and tenacity could make money by ferreting around in shops such as this.

"Does your friend collect anything in particular?"

"Not really. I'm hoping something will catch my eye."

She made a broad sweep of the room anticipating that something would jump out. Her purchase had to be small so she looked to the random collections of objects on horizontal surfaces. Would these objects normally sit together in a home, she wondered? On a small bamboo table by the side of the woman, she saw a pot— simple and matte, almost pewter colored, just twelve centimeters high, a truncated cone with two angular handles attached at the rim and halfway down the slope of the cone. It was an Upchurch pot, hand-thrown, Arts and Crafts, early twentieth century, worth the equivalent of one month's salary for Dave. She looked at the base. Yes, it was Upchurch but valued correctly, unfortunately.

She moved around the room recognizing and then rejecting each fairly priced and each over-priced object in turn. There were five potential purchases she had to reject; they were too cumbersome, too fragile or too difficult to sell-on. This was not as easy as she'd imagined. Had she allowed sufficient time? In the corner of the room, farthest from the entrance, she noticed a tangle of jewelry crammed together as though the shop owner conceded that no single item had any particular merit. Jayna poked around among the tacky oddments.

"I have regulars who always buy a bit of something from that pile. You might find a present there. It's all costume jewelry but it's fun."

"This is sweet," said Jayna. Her heartbeat leapt. The brooch, thanks to decades of grime, merged easily with the neighboring tat, but there was no doubt: square, cut corners, with cobalt and white enamel stripes, a narrow checkerboard border. And, on the reverse, the impressed monogram, WW, just discernible: Wiener Werkstätte. There was little intrinsic value in the enamel or its copper base but Jayna had learnt that the lowliest materials could be transformed into an object of desire. She could see the hand of the designer (she was sure it was Josef Hoffmann) and she imagined him checking the brooch, handling it, turning it over, making sure it matched his intentions. Dave would survive for three months on this. Jayna walked to the counter. "I'll take it."

"I'll knock a bit off for a new customer." And she dropped the brooch into a small paper bag.

"Thanks. I'll be sure to come again." She slipped the tiny packet into her pocket. Perfect. Wiener Werkstätte—so easy to miss and so very easy to sell.

Reaching the edge of the terminal piazza fifteen minutes too early for her shuttle, she sat on the front edge of a bench that was already burning hot from the morning sun. She held the brooch in her pocket and breathed deeply, steadily; impatient now. People criss-crossed around her. Their pace was relaxed and they wore less formal clothing than during the week. As she sizzled in the sunshine, her eyes were drawn to an elderly man standing incongruously at the center of the piazza. He wore a pinstriped suit that would surely have been his most expensive item of clothing at some time in the past. The jacket hung slightly off center, making his shoulders appear inadequate and she imagined how twenty years ago his frame and bulkier muscles would have better matched the suit's size and former elegance. And with a sharper haircut and polished shoes, he'd have projected the image of a confident, even strutting, corporate executive.

He removed a bag from his trouser pocket and dropped seeds at his feet. The signal was detected and an army of sparrows and pigeons massed around him. There he stood, unflinching, as the birds clambered over his feet in their frenzy. The simple fact that he dropped the seeds, instead of throwing them a few feet away, marked him out. He let the birds scramble across his shoes; feathers touched the fabric of his shiny suit. It didn't take much to delineate madness. She felt edgy. And for a few seconds, she re-read the scene before her. No longer was the man demonstrating an act of kindness towards pathetic beggars. No, these birds had merely broken their carefree flight across the metropolis on an impulse. They probably were not even hungry. The solitary male figure needed them far more than they needed him. It was all a matter of perception. Passers-by checked him out. A group of teenagers sneered and, in the next instant, he was banished from their thoughts.

With five minutes to the shuttle departure, she set off towards the terminus, crossed the concourse, and strode towards the platform. Much as she longed to see Dave once again, she was equally eager for the shuttle trip. In fact, the journey would transform her mindset into a perfect state of readiness for meeting him. The open spaces, the big horizons. Anyone witnessing so much sky, she thought, must experience…must actually feel free, alive, physically. She felt it now; it was a tingly and light sensation. But this quickening was soon arrested as she took her seat in the grungy carriage. These long-horizon feelings were a trick, she decided. *Our emotions kid us that life is better than the sum of its unremarkable parts.* She cast her thoughts back to the old man in his weary suit. *Our delusions are our best defense.*

As the shuttle picked up speed through the inner suburbs, she imagined the homely interiors that streaked past. Some, no doubt, would be even more beautiful than the Slaters'. She imagined themes for different living spaces and she scattered through them, on the thinnest of floating glass shelves, many of the antiques she'd just seen and touched, creating multiple fantasies of domestic perfection. What would her favorite theme be, she wondered? As though her mind were stuck in a groove, she was drawn once again to the accoutrements of coffee making—starting with an array of traditional grinders. *I'd collect coffee cups whenever I went on holiday. Even better, I'd photograph interesting cups of coffee served to me in spectacular settings, or photograph Dave drinking coffee. And, definitely, cups of coffee shot from above—before and after—showing the perfect frothy milk toppings next to the drained cups with their subtle staining. They'd look pretty restrained. I'd hang the photos on muted gray walls. I can just see it…too much of one thing though. A sub-theme to act as a foil; not a complete contrast, just something that picks out one aspect of the coffee idea and inverts it in some way. Something that contrasts with the harsh shiny surfaces of crockery, more textured and battered—driftwood or old furniture. Or perhaps I should offset the mass-produced character of the crockery with hand-made earthy ceramics. The Upchurch would be so perfect. Then a couple of textile pieces to soften the overall ceramic concept. I can see myself in the room. I'm wearing chalky-green, baggy trousers and a frayed, white T-shirt and I'm a foil myself to the crisp aesthetic of the photographs. Just so.*

She awaited the sharp transition between the suburbs and farm territories and when the shuttle crossed the boundary she gaped. And she continued to gape as the shuttle passed through the first enclaves. Less shocked this time by the squat, featureless town-scapes, she noticed more clearly the emergence of citrus groves that she knew stretched westwards, out to the Welsh mountains. She tried to name the varieties but the speed of the shuttle smudged her attempts into guesses. Who would have thought, she mused, that citrus would find a home, here, so far from China? And two sentences of prose trickled across her thoughts, written thousands of years before: *The baskets were filled with woven ornamental silks. The bundle contained small oranges and pummeloes.*

C. medica (citron), C. grandis or C. maxima (pummelo), C. reticulata (mandarin/tangerine), and C. aurantiifolia (lime). There are just four ancestral genetic species for the entire gamut of citrus that spread across the globe from China and South East Asia. The lack of any sterility barrier between varieties has resulted in countless wild and cultivated hybrids.

She listed some of the crossings: citron and lime crossing to become the lemon; pummelo and mandarin forming both the sour orange and the sweet orange (an odd fact, she thought); then, the sweet orange combining with its progenitor, the pummelo, to make the grapefruit, and with its other progenitor, the mandarin, to form the tangor; grapefruit and mandarin crossing to make the tangelo (the variant Jamaican tangelo known unkindly as the Ugli fruit); mandarin and lime forming the Chinese lemon…

A vast and intimate family, she thought, or total breeding chaos.

———

Dave lifted his arm and spread his palm wide in salutation. The thrill of recognition sent needles shooting down from her neck, through her arms and her hands, and out through her fingertips. She offered a handshake as he approached, and gestured backward with her head in the direction of another passenger who had alighted. "Keep it formal. Just in case."

"Okay, but tell me, Jayna, *what's* going on? That's all bank account stuff in that file, isn't it?"

Ignoring his question she said, "My friend Veronica was taken away on Friday."

"Who? Is she…same as you?"

She nodded. "Let's walk through the market and then we'll be okay to go back to your place."

He brushed his hand against hers. "Jayna, what are you up to?"

She looked across the expanse of derelict car park towards the housing blocks. She would attempt to explain everything before they reached the packed streets. "Things aren't looking good. We could be on the verge of a complete recall. The Constructor must be getting nervous…At the very least, random checks might start and I reckon I'd soon come to their notice."

"Why's that?"

"It sounds stupid but my stick insects are a bit of an anomaly. And our canteen assistant might decide to say something."

"What about?"

"That I'm more interested in the food than the other residents are."

"Doesn't sound like much."

"I know. But it could be enough. And, I lied to my friends about last weekend and that may be picked up if the Constructor really starts checking." She pressed on. "So…I've been siphoning money from several bank accounts, buying shares. It's all detailed in the Sarcophagus file."

"Jesus!" He barked a laugh. "How much?"

"Plenty."

He picked up a stone and threw it, with all his strength, high into the air.

"Dave, don't attract attention."

"Can you get away with it?"

"Please, Dave. Listen. I know it sounds impossible but I have to disappear, away from the city. I want to hide out in the enclaves, permanently."

"What, with me? Wouldn't they make the connection? You visiting today…"

"No. I don't want to implicate you in any of this. I'll disappear somewhere else and when it's safe, if you want to, we can make contact."

"But where, Jayna? You don't know your way around."

"I've got some help…He's already set up a safe house."

Dave stopped, and turned to her. "*He*? Who's *he*?"

"Another simulant. Sunjin, from C6. He works for the Metropolitan Police and wants out. He's the one who told me about Veronica; found me on Friday and he's really upset. He took a huge risk approaching me." She hoped this would placate him. "And Sunjin even told me the address of his safe house. But you can see, Dave, if he's already figured me out then others will too."

He fell quiet and kicked, or rather stubbed, a stone upwards. It followed a steep arc and fell into the center of a discarded tire. "This is getting fucking complicated. Can you trust this guy?"

"I think so. I have to now."

"Look, Jayna, I've had enough of Mayhew McCline. You know that. And if you can pull this off…with the money…"

"I'm getting bio data from Sunjin, for the bank accounts. What about—?"

"It's okay. I removed the Sarcophagus file from Mayhew McCline. I've deleted the file from the tower. I didn't want to keep it at home either so I've found a safe place—"

"Don't tell me for now."

"Right."

"It's all happening quicker than I expected."

"So when are you…?"

"It's unbelievable…but I think soon. It's just too risky to delay. Sunjin and I will have to disappear at the same time. So Saturday, ideally. And then, after a while you can join us, if you decide that's what you want. Or, we'll come and find you."

"I'll just walk out of Mayhew McCline?"

"I've thought about that. You should get yourself sacked for bad time-keeping. Or pick an argument with someone like Hester. She'd demand dismissal."

"Yeah, that would work. They'd just forget about me then."

"But you have to be sure about this. You'll be out of a job, no company—"

Dave jerked into defense mode. Three dogs were bolting towards them from the housing blocks. He pulled Jayna behind him. Stooped to grab a handful of grit. The dogs were racing closer, ears back. He crouched with arms and legs spread wide, ready to match the dogs' speed with aggression. But they veered off, more intent on escaping their tormentors than facing a new confrontation. He dropped the detritus and brushed his hands against his trousers.

"Come on," she said. "Let's get going."

They entered the enclave proper.

"You'll need a plan beyond the safe house, y'know," said Dave.

"Sunjin will decide how long we can stay there."

"I'm the one with the local know-how. I reckon you and Sunjin could disappear among the farm migrants almost indefinitely. You could do that till things calm down. And I'd be a free agent so I could set something up. I'd need a bit of money, though." He stopped as though he'd remembered something important. "What exactly is the deal with this Sunjin?"

"He doesn't know anything about you, yet. I didn't want to say anything until I'd spoken with you first." She walked on but he hadn't finished. "So, this guy thinks he's doing a runner with *you*. *You* and *him*?"

"Not like that. He just wants out."

At which point, they began to merge with the enclave residents who were milling around in the less-frenetic Sunday market. They kept their uneasy thoughts to themselves and became just another pair of friends, seemingly with nothing more to do than browse the pavement stalls, with no more on their minds than who they might meet later in the day and where they might hang out.

"I'd love to live here, Dave."

He didn't want to laugh at her but he did. "You don't know what you're talking about, do you? I guarantee you'd change your mind within forty-eight hours."

"Quite likely. Right now, I'm fed up pretending I'm fact-finding for Mayhew McCline."

"Fine by me. There's a short cut, half-way down Clothing Street." He set a faster pace dodging in and around the shoppers but it was still slow going. Ahead of them, a refuse collector emerged from a side street to the left, pedaling and sweating; his puny body barely capable of propelling his mountainous load forward. Remembering the stench, she covered her mouth and nose as he turned towards them. The sweating man leaned forward and, lifting his face, caught Jayna's eye.

In a split second, the crowd froze en masse. A male voice roared out of the side street and a short, stocky figure tore across Clothing Street. He threw himself bodily at the refuse collector. Both men sprawled through the paralyzed shoppers and crashed to the ground at Jayna's feet. Dave pushed her backwards against other shoppers. Children were grabbed by parents. Everyone jostled to get away from the fist-fight. Two blurs, a man and a woman, charged out of the side street and they piled in.

"Move back," barked Dave. He pushed her towards the side street but she strained to look back over her shoulder. She caught sight of bloodied fists.

"Knives!" a woman screamed. Dave grabbed Jayna's arm and as they turned into the side street another man shot past. He tore into the fight, threw badly aimed punches. A whistle pierced the air—once, twice, three times.

"Jayna, hurry for Christ's sake. Police will be all over the place soon."

They stumbled down the side street. She shook with excitement. "That's a real fight!"

A man looked out from a doorway, thirty meters farther along, and yelled to Dave: "What's going on up there?"

He shouted back: "Don't go up there, mate. It's another punch-up over the bloody rubbish." They reached the man. Dave put his hand on the man's shoulder. "Getting beyond a joke, this."

"Where's the police?"

"Scratching their arses," said Dave. And they both laughed.

"Hey, come in." Dave took Jayna's hand and stepped through the entrance. The man stood back to let them pass but she was hesitant. "You all right?" said the man. She nodded.

"Pretty dramatic," said Dave. "It happened right in front of us. They'll be looking for witnesses if anyone's knifed." Dave squeezed Jayna's hand as his friend led the way. "Better keeping off the streets for a while."

This building was darker than Dave's and the passageway was narrow. His friend lived on the ground floor at the back of the building. An unpleasant smell. Like the smell in a pet shop. As his friend shoved obstructions out of the way, muttering to himself, Dave spoke quietly to Jayna: "It's a detour, I know. But we've got enough time…you'll find Leo's place interesting." He kissed her cheek. "Another wee enterprise."

They stepped into his noxious flat and while Dave made the introductions, Jayna tried to work out what she was looking at and frowned. "What on Earth…?" she murmured. A fly zapper, with its glaring blue light, hung disturbingly close to eye level from the low ceiling. It was suspended above a metal tray that was clearly acting as a chute directed towards a huge tank of bubbling water, two cubic meters she reckoned. And there were pipes—the water was being aerated.

Zap! A fly dropped into the tank. She stepped forward, peered in and saw fish. She laughed, captivated.

"I said you'd like it," said Dave. She looked at Leo for some explanation.

"Obviously, I have to live on the ground floor with this lot."

"Obviously. But is it allowed?"

"I haven't asked. I don't think I'd like the answer."

Dave stepped forward. "Leo's a foreman at the fish farm— y'know, next to the generation plant." She did know. All the enclaves had the same set-up; power from waste with the fisheries sited alongside. They shared a pool of bonded labor and the whole enterprise helped to keep running costs low for the enclaves.

"I used to supervise labor on the gray side of the generation plant—shoveling ash, making bricks. But now I watch over the fishery, spend most of my time at the tanks."

"Is there any violence?" she asked, the street fight fresh in her mind.

"Nah. They're just refugees working on right-to-stay rules. It's a cushy number for them, especially working with the fish."

"Leo knows everything about carp farming," said Dave, evidently proud of his association.

"I'll make us a cup of tea then, shall I?"

She walked around the tank working out the sums for Leo's little earner. Few fixed overheads; minimal rent, free electricity, free labor. "Are these insects enough for them?" She assumed not.

"No, the insects are like fresh supplements." He grinned. "I bring fish food and antibiotic solution back from the works. It's a tiny amount, relatively. No one notices."

"But the smell? Does no one mind?"

"Not if I keep everyone well supplied. You'll notice the kids in this building are pretty healthy looking."

She turned to Dave. "Remember you told me last Saturday about cooking fish. Did you mean Leo's fish?" He nodded.

"Second date then," said Leo, mashing the mint tea.

They ignored him. "The tea smells good," said Jayna.

"Best thing in this heat, with this smell. You can actually taste something." And he passed around the small glasses.

"Slurp it, to cool it down," said Dave, and Leo demonstrated. Jayna broke into a fit of giggles. Mistakenly, she thought he was exaggerating for comic effect. They stood around the tank, watched the carp writhe around each other while Jayna did her best to imitate Leo's eccentric manners.

———

"Tell me about the fight," she said as soon as they left Leo's flat. "What was that all about?"

"That guy who was attacked? He was on their patch most likely."

"They have patches?"

"Yes. It's developed over the years along with the aggravation. Individual groups, mostly families, bought the rights to collect rubbish along individual streets. And families are passing on the rights to sons and daughters."

"Was that the original intention?"

"No. They were supposed to re-apply every five years for the collection rights. But the housing department couldn't be bothered with the admin cost, so that's how it evolved."

"So one family per street?"

"Roughly speaking. The streets run the length of the enclave and there's rich pickings if they can stop any encroachment."

"People try to steal rubbish?"

"Why not? Just another commodity."

She retracted into her own thoughts as they continued through dusty streets towards Dave's block, then piped up: "It sounds exactly like the old problem with the vineyards…in Burgundy."

"What?" said Dave. He'd completely lost the thread.

"Well, the Burgundy wines were produced by monks in the Middle Ages but when their power started to wane, many of the vineyards were sold off to private owners. Then along came the Napoleonic Inheritance Laws that said private property had to be split equally among siblings. From that point on these incredibly valuable lands were subdivided—" she looked at Dave to see if he followed her drift "—*again* and *again* until, at the end of the last century, each family often owned a single row of vines. So a single row of vines could end up having its own label."

"I don't think any of our rubbish will get a label."

She smiled. "What I mean, Dave, is this: it's not sustainable to keep the rubbish business within the family. They realized that eventually in the vineyards. But it's a nice story."

He put his arm round her. "A nice story? You're becoming quite a romantic."

———

Climbing the stairs to his flat, she still had the Burgundians in mind as she once again traced the wall's history with her fingertips. *History lends character*, she thought as she reached the second floor.

That's the heart of my problem. I haven't lived enough. My character is just the combination of my intellect and my faults. I haven't had time to become more complex, more interesting. As she stepped inside the flat ahead of Dave, she turned to face him. "I'm not sure if you realize this but without my flaws I'd be pretty dull. You should know that."

He took her face in both hands. "That goes for everyone, you idiot."

One hour and seven minutes later, they dressed. They sat at Dave's small table, which he had laid out with olives, misshapen tomatoes, and heavy unleavened bread. The heat had been so stifling that after their love-making, he'd led Jayna to stand in front of the shuttered windows to catch the breeze blowing through half-opened slats. He'd soaked a towel at his sink and wiped her down, and she'd reciprocated.

He now watched her eating. "You know, I could cope with Mayhew McCline if we could come home to one another."

"Hmm, that would be lovely."

He guessed that the word *lovely* was addressed to the olives as much as his remark. "You're a bit obsessive about food, aren't you?"

"This is the best meal I have ever had." She sat back to give Dave her complete attention and added carefully: "I love knowing that you've shopped in the market and chosen this food especially for me, for us; that, when you bought the olives, you were thinking about me, and about what I might like."

"It's true. That's exactly how it was."

"And I was thinking of you when I bought this earlier today." She set the tiny package on the table.

"What's this?"

"A present. Or, more precisely, an investment."

He unwrapped the object. "Is it worth something?"

"Worth forty times what I paid." Dave inspected the label and maker's mark on the back. "I decided you needed a fallback…if things unravel. I'm concerned…"

"You don't need to be, Jayna. All the same, thanks. Thanks a lot."

"With the money you make on this you'll have time to think. Maybe you can start a small business here in the enclave. If you want to."

"A second-hand book stall?"

"Well, possibly. That would be fun. But don't forget, Dave, people don't need to buy books but they do need to buy food."

He reached for her hand.

"Wait, give me a pen." She flattened the discarded paper bag and took the pen from his hand. "You'll need this, too."

"What?"

"The maker and designer of the brooch, and the address of our safe house."

"Right. So…I'll meet you there if…I mean when you disappear, when you don't come to work."

"That's right. Leave it a few days though."

He turned the brooch over. "They'd go ballistic at the office if they knew about you and me."

"I want you to remember something, Dave. I don't blame Mayhew McCline for this mess I'm in. They didn't know what to expect when I turned up."

"But if you were recalled, could Olivia refuse to hand you over?"

"I think she'd try."

"I'm not convinced, Jayna. It's business. They only fucking care about profits. They'd just accept a replacement."

"I'm sure Benjamin would want me back. He was lovely with his family. He seemed very caring."

"But if it all goes wrong and you *are* recalled, do you think Olivia and Benjamin could get you back from the Constructor?"

"No, I don't."

CHAPTER 15

Adead stick insect in its shroud, a feather, a bare twig, and three olive stones; not a random collection at all. They were all part of the natural world, or they had been. She held them loosely in her pocket as she headed downtown from the shuttle terminus. *A clear pattern,* she thought. *I suppose the first artifact was so...evocative, I was drawn to similar things; objects that pressed the same buttons.* She made slight adjustments to the length of her stride so that every seventh footfall crossed a joint in the paving flags. A small stone lay on the ground just ahead of her and she stubbed it with her right foot, mimicking Dave's skilful move in the car park. But instead of lifting in an arc towards the manhole cover she'd spotted a few meters away, it sliced sideways with considerable energy so that it came to rest in the middle of the road.

She walked alongside the park where, for the past three months, every Monday afternoon, she'd fed the pigeons. An innocent routine but she now wondered if it marked something else, maybe an unconscious fall-out in her behavior. She put her hand to her forehead as though checking her temperature. Dozens of questions vied for attention. But one question beat all others into submission. Was anyone else planning to escape? Because the tipping point was grossly apparent: as soon as one of her generation made a run for it, they would all be recalled. The pavement became crowded as several main streets converged on the Entertainment

Quarter. She looked down as though sensing that people could read her thoughts: she and Sunjin *had* to be the first runaways. Involuntarily, nerve endings activated and shimmered in her arms, back, neck, and the sides of her face, lingering on her cheekbones. A few strides on, she jaywalked the final junction. No, she decided, it wasn't *fear* she was feeling. It was simply the uncertainty, *not knowing*. It came down to this: there would be a passage of time from this point until the final outcome, and there was no knowing how it would turn out. It simply wasn't decided yet. She would make certain moves but only the end result would decide whether her moves were well judged. She murmured, "Everything will come to pass."

Jayna approached the Repertory Domes and sighed heavily; the Domes demanded enthusiasm. On reaching the entrance she fixed a smile and swiped her season ticket. There ought to be a warning: *No Inhibitions Tolerated*. On Sunday afternoons, the two smaller Repertory Domes sucked in child starlets while adult wannabees headed for the giant Dome at the far end of the complex. She skirted the piazza, stopped at a popcorn vendor, and reluctantly exchanged half her remaining funds for their smallest offering. She wasn't hungry in the least; she simply wanted a prop.

The Dome was already abuzz with the warm-up entertainment—a fairly shambolic line-up of have-a-go lesser talents. This was Jayna's favorite part of the event, less serious, more of a backdrop, making it easier to chat while lounging around. However, Jayna's friends did not lounge as convincingly as neighboring groups; they couldn't sit cock-eyed. There was no flailing of arms or legs over the arms of chairs or sofas. Equally, though, they never looked with envy, as their neighbors did, at those lucky people on the balconies around the dome's inner circumference, closer to the stars twinkling in the planetarium overhead.

Jayna paused inside the Dome's entrance. The grandeur of the auditorium had always appealed to her and now she realized why. The structure dwarfed the audience, dominated them, so that any differences between individuals seemed to diminish to insignificance. Even so, she thought, she wouldn't mind if she never saw this place again. She spotted her friends and waved. She had to be convincing. Several hands shot up in response. A waiter was setting drinks down on their table.

"Get your drink order in, Jayna," said Lucas.

"Orange juice, please. No ice." She handed the popcorn to Harry. "Help yourselves." He took a single piece and passed the carton along.

"How was your trip, then?" said Harry, as she dropped into the sofa.

"Interesting, I suppose. Glad to get back really. I'm exhausted."

"Well...tell us later. It can wait." The popcorn went full circle and she regained possession.

"So what's happening here?" she said.

"We're trying to persuade Julie to get up and sing before the competition starts," said Lucas.

"Okay, okay," said Julie. "I will, now that Jayna's here." As Julie stood and straightened her clothes, Jayna started to smile but her mouth distorted into a small grimace. Julie picked her way through the early arrivals to the center of the Dome where she joined the performers' queue. She looked back towards her friends who waved in support.

"They'll think the competition has begun once Julie starts to sing," said Lucas.

But Jayna wasn't listening. That sickly feeling had returned and she placed the flat of her hand against her gut and swallowed her saliva. She gazed across at Julie standing patiently in line. Jayna credited her nausea to a single fact: she didn't need Julie as much as Julie seemed to need her. It wasn't exactly a feeling of disdain, she admitted to herself; she felt faintly...*repelled* by her friend's keen attachment. *Am I corrupted? I used to be a good person.*

"There they are," called Lucas. The C6 simulants entered the Dome and Jayna realized they would bring news of Veronica. Julie would be the last to find out. Sunjin maneuvered within the group as they approached. He aimed to be on her side of the gathering when the two groups met. Harry and Lucas set about reorganizing sofas and chairs so they could all sit around two low tables. And, in the hesitancy and politeness of their arrival, Jayna stepped towards Sunjin so they could sit together at the end of arrangement. Once settled, the news about Veronica came out, not in a burst, or in the furtive manner of Sunjin's announcement to Jayna on Friday. In fact, they seemed to small-talk their way through Veronica's disappearance.

"Have you heard anything at all about the reason?" said Harry.

"Well, it only happened on Friday," said Sunjin. "Maybe we'll hear something tomorrow when we all get back to work."

"She might be back at work herself," said Jayna.

"I suppose we shouldn't jump to conclusions," said Harry.

"No, we shouldn't," said Jayna. "There's no point speculating."

Nevertheless a few tentative suggestions were put forward and she took the opportunity, when the conversation was concentrated at the far end of the group, to speak to Sunjin. She held a piece of popcorn close to her face to obscure her mouth from the others. And she delivered a précis on the subject of Dave including his address, his possession of specific information. Evidently, Sunjin was beyond being shocked. He, in turn, took a piece of popcorn and spoke in staccato. He'd been into police headquarters both mornings. The bio data was pretty much sorted. There ought to be pre-existing supplies at the safe house—food, clothes, and a little cash.

A birdsong impressionist stepped on stage and seized everyone's attention, except Jayna's and Sunjin's.

"Does anyone at headquarters know about the house?" said Jayna.

"It's been a long time since anyone's been there. I faked a demolition order when I heard about Veronica, and the building details were struck from our files. Don't think anyone will notice."

When the impressionist stopped chirruping, Harry caught Jayna's eye. "What do you think, Jayna? Veronica seemed perfectly fine last Sunday."

She shrugged. "Yes she did. It's all a mystery to me. Veronica's a perfect employee as far as I can tell. But I suppose in her kind of work, results are difficult to quantify."

"You have a point there. Maybe they couldn't justify the cost," said Harry. This neatly deflected their concern since, if Harry were correct, Veronica might well reappear, if not in her current post then elsewhere in the city with a new employer.

Ahead of them, Julie took center stage—a small figure, a child standing forlorn at the center of a playground, arms by her side. Few people took notice. As the music struck up, Jayna leaned closer to Sunjin and they continued their dark murmurings. And Julie sang a poetic ballad well known to the audience, a song usually belted out carelessly. So her measured rendition, perfectly pitched, tickled the crowd's curiosity. At the end of the first verse, with a flick of a switch backstage, Julie's face appeared on the battery of giant screens around the Dome. The audience applauded, concurring with the management's decision. Her singing was surely as sweet as anything they would hear that afternoon.

At the start of the second verse, Julie was still abandoned in the playground, almost unmoving. But slowly, just perceptibly, her body started to sway and as she hit the chorus for a second time she allowed her head to tip back as she mimicked the facial contortions of some great diva. She hiked the volume. The crowds cheered and whistled as they recognized the transformation, one they all craved in their own karaoke. They all wanted to be as good as this nobody.

Even Jayna was dragged out of conversation. "This should be Julie's life," she said under her breath. How could one of her friends be so appealing to all these people? She surveyed the punters sitting nearby—their eyes flicked from one screen to another. The performance could be genuine, she thought. Had Julie stretched

her emotions by faking them? Or was her fakery only a part of
it? Perhaps she physically experienced something when she sang.
The two elements might have combined. At the final chorus, the
crowd became raucous. Their shout-singing threatened to drown
Julie's perfect delivery. But her rich and textured voice prevailed and
wrapped the crooners in a warm and generous sensuality.

Jayna turned away from Julie and finalized her dealings with
Sunjin: "So, we're ready?"

He nodded. "I'll sort out the loose ends tomorrow." The crowds
hurled their applause towards the screens and Jayna marveled at the
understated pleasure in her friends' faces.

"It's definitely Saturday?" he asked.

She hesitated, then, "Yes, immediately after breakfast. No one
will notice until the evening."

Julie was walking back and Sunjin stood to applaud her arrival.
"Did you like it?" she said looking directly at Sunjin.

"Your best effort yet," he said. Julie approached him and reached
out. She slipped her hands around Sunjin's waist. Jayna leapt forward and pulled her by the arm. "You were completely brilliant."
And twisted her away from Sunjin, pushing her towards an empty
sofa. The next performance was starting and attention was diverted.
"What in heaven's name are you doing, Julie?"

"I don't see—"

"Just don't."

———

As she rinsed her hands at the basin in her room, Jayna realized she'd
taken far longer over her pre-dining ablutions than necessary. But
slowly, in turn, she continued to pull each hand through the clutch
of the other and she felt soothed by the running water and the feel
of skin on skin. So much had happened today. She wanted to slow
her mind and this rhythmic movement steadied her thoughts. Was

it possible to comfort oneself, she wondered? Jayna recalled a small fiction she'd created while lying with Dave earlier in the day. Jayna had faced away from him without any part of their bodies touching. And he'd stroked her hair. For a moment she'd imagined the soft pressure on her hair being applied by another hand, not Dave's. She didn't know who she wanted that other person to be.

She dropped the coarse hand towel, sat on the edge of her bed, and massaged her forehead with her fingertips. Soothing, but not comforting. She tried something else; she leaned the side of her face into her left palm, as though nursing a toothache, and stroked above her right eyebrow, slowly, from the bridge of her nose around to her temple, with the fingertips of her free hand.

Footsteps in the corridor; they jolted her. And a knock.

"Mind if I catch you before dinner?" It was Julie. She looked at the discarded towel on the floor. Jayna hastily picked it up. "Sure, there's no rush."

Julie leaned back against the door. Her face looked flushed. "I was excited…about the singing. It went so well, I thought. I just wanted to…I don't know. Sunjin looked so happy for me."

"Don't worry. I don't think anyone realized what you were doing."

"You won't mention anything over dinner?"

"Of course I won't, Julie."

And with that, Julie turned to leave. She hesitated and appeared to speak to the door. "I'm not going to sing any more. I'll keep away from the karaoke."

———

"I'm beginning to feel like a human guinea pig with all these menu changes," said Lucas over dinner.

"They don't use guinea pigs anymore," said Jayna tersely, "but the phrase has stuck."

"If you said that in parts of South America, Lucas, they might misunderstand. Guinea pigs are a delicacy. They would think you were making some reference to cannibalism," said Harry. The small group of friends threw glances at one another but appeared unable to propel the conversation on guinea pigs any further. They returned to their meals.

Why had Lucas used such an archaic phrase in the first place? Jayna was frustrated with him. And what exactly did he imagine he was if he wasn't a human guinea pig? He just didn't see it. But maybe he could be pushed from the straight path, she thought, if he stumbled across a set of circumstances, if he found himself in a certain place at a certain time, if someone said a particular something or if he was subjected to a specific physical experience. It was feasible that a combination of such incidents could launch an uncharacteristic and original thought. All her friends might come to their senses, eventually. Maybe the revelation, if she could call it that, had simply come to her sooner rather than later.

The subject of Veronica had been exhausted on the way home from the Repertory Domes and no one was eager to resurrect the discussion. Julie kept her head down. It was Harry who opened a new conversation: "Jayna, what about the enclave. How did it go?"

She refocused. "It wasn't exactly what I expected."

"More surprises?"

"What do you mean, *more?*"

"Well, you were surprised by your afternoon at Benjamin's."

"You're right…I can say this much: I think I've learnt something this weekend, Harry. Information is not the same as knowledge."

"Care to elaborate?"

"I thought I knew a great deal about the enclaves—when they were built, who lives there, demographics, how housing policies have changed, transport links, employment statistics—but it doesn't amount to much. There's a gap, you see. A shuttle timetable doesn't tell you, for example, that the carriages are uncomfortable. You only gain that knowledge by taking a shuttle journey."

"Was that the main surprise?" asked Julie, making an effort to join in.

"No." She forced a smile. "It was the enclave itself. It was so basic, so drab, nothing remotely like the suburbs. And yet... bustling with life."

"More so than the suburbs?" said Harry.

"I didn't see anyone walking around in Benjamin's area. I expect they were all indoors or in their gardens. But in the enclaves accommodation is cramped. They don't have private gardens and there are no open spaces for recreation as far as I could see. Everyone seems to be in the street. And the streets are so dusty. Another thing... there are no shops as such. They buy everything at market stalls. I didn't realize that. Do you see what I mean? I knew the breakdown of business types based on the traders' licenses but I didn't realize they operated from makeshift tables set out along the streets and—"

"If yer want yer lemon tart," shouted the canteen assistant from behind his counter, "yer'd better get up 'ere fast. It's startin' t'look a bit sad." They looked at one another and pushed their chairs back. Jayna didn't get up.

Once they returned to the table Julie picked up the conversation again: "It all sounds chaotic in the enclaves."

"It's full of life, that's for sure. Children kick about in the streets enjoying themselves. But if their surroundings were a little more pleasant..." She wasn't going to tell them about the fight.

"We don't believe at our department that—"

"Yes, I know you think they have a fair deal, Harry. I came away feeling, apart from anything else, they didn't have much opportunity to better themselves."

"Do they want to?" asked Lucas.

She wasn't getting the reaction she wanted at all. "Of course they do." She leaned back. "They're not morons."

Julie and Lucas looked alarmed. "They may not be," Harry intervened, "but it doesn't necessarily follow they want more. They get a good deal and they know it. You know it."

"It's not really a question of getting more. Maybe the state should…back off a bit. Stop pigeonholing everyone. Just let them breathe a bit."

They gawped at her. She stood up and raised her palms towards them. "Look. I've had a very tiring day. I'm obviously not explaining myself very well. Let's talk tomorrow when my head's clear."

———

Jayna leaned back against her door and tapped her head backwards. "I'm the moron," she murmured. Five days more…And, as if one anxiety naturally spawned another anxiety, she felt a shiver of concern for Sunjin. He hadn't *been* to the enclaves. He was nowhere near as street-wise as he'd like to think.

Tomorrow, she would download all the data she could find on Enclaves W3 and W8, GPS data, plus all the timetables, route-planners. "And what about you?" she said, peering at her stick insects, which hung from the top of the mesh cage. "Who's going to look after you?" She sprayed a mist of water across the vegetation and she smiled. Breaking the rules was something they had in common.

Dollo's Law of Evolution: Complex structures cannot return to a condition seen in an ancestor; a law overturned by the humble stick insect. Even when stick insects lose their wings during their evolutionary history, they keep the genes for making them. They have lost and regained their wings several times over the millennia.

She made a plan for her little friends: stock up on greenery during the coming week, pick up a business card from the florist and leave it by the cage. Julie would see it. *Yes, I expect you'll end*

up with Julie…And all the data I've collected, it would be a waste.
Perhaps I should send everything to Bangalore. But she dismissed the
idea. There were too many other things to think about. She set out
the new ground rules: no unnecessary conversation with anyone at
C7 or at work, take the usual route to the office, feed the pigeons
after work, no contact with Dave, absolutely none. And she meant
it this time. She'd send a bland report to Benjamin and Olivia on
her trip to the enclave making non-committal comments but giving
the impression that further research might not be worthwhile. Then
Olivia might step in and encourage her to drop the whole thing.
And, reluctantly she would concur, but she would ask to keep the
file open for future investigation. Then, everything calm on the surface, she and Sunjin could set out separately, on Saturday, as easily
as she'd visited Dave.

The lights faded. She dressed her wooden chair with her clothes.
As she floated towards sleep, sometimes dipping under but then
resurfacing, she saw a long ticker tape. It swirled in eddies. Words
were handwritten along the entire length: *leaves on a tree like sticks*
on a twig like clothes on a chair like leaves on a tree like sticks on…
At last, she slipped below the surface and drowned into sleep, into a
dream that served, as ever, to purge, shuffle, and juxtapose the day's
events, before spewing crazed stories that, surely, she could never
have imagined in waking hours. She was in a field. From a tangle of
vines that towered above her head, Jayna tore over-ripe, rotting, and
distended fruits. She discarded them all. Her feet slid on the mush
as she pulled, arching backwards, for hours it seemed. All night. In
her dream she wanted vine leaves for her insects. She had to have
them. Her arms were lacerated and she tried to shout: *Where are the*
leaves? There are no leaves. But the words would not leave the back of
her throat. They could not reach her straining mouth.

CHAPTER 16

A percussive sound—a door had hit its jamb, or a window had struck its frame. It broke her dream. She woke with her mouth still straining and she knew she had tried to shout out. Relieved to be awake, she pushed herself up on one elbow and for a few moments felt the lacerations on her arms. She raised herself to her feet and felt an urge to swill her face for she wanted to wake up fully—the dream might otherwise keep its grip. But before she reached the sink she registered (a) faint, untidy noises somewhere within the rest station and (b) the gritty sound of footsteps outside. Too early for the recycling gang; Monday wasn't their day anyway. It was curiosity rather than concern that prompted Jayna to move towards the window.

On the corner of the street, on the opposite pavement, stood a bald-headed man in neat, dark clothing. He looked along Granby Row, first in one direction, then the other. He turned 180 degrees and stared directly at the rest station's side entrance, below and to the left of Jayna's window. Why would he look over here, she wondered? He twisted back and waved, striding out into the junction. Waiting for a lift? It was an odd, in-between place to arrange a pick-up. She checked the time: 06:58 hours. Her jaw ached.

The slight sound of a vehicle. It swung slowly round and pulled up by the side entrance. The man ran from the junction and opened the rear passenger door. She pushed her face against the window to see more. A familiar sound: the side entrance doors being un-locked and opened, but thirty minutes earlier than usual. A shuffle of people, two men and between them a smaller…"Julie!" Jayna raised her fists and banged against the window frame. They eased Julie into the back seat—she didn't struggle—and the vehicle rolled quietly away. Jayna's eyes burned down the empty street. Was her mind playing games? *Did Julie really twist around? Did she? Did our eyes meet?*

Was it the singing? They didn't like the singing? Or…the email to Sunjin? He didn't delete it? Did he report her? Jayna lifted her hands to cover her face, to hide from premonitions. *Too late. I've said too much. Julie won't think to keep quiet.*

But Jayna had already focused on the important fact: the side entrance was unlocked. She began to pull on her clothes. The streets and the Southern Terminus would be quieter now than in an hour's time; too quiet maybe. *And, Sunjin! What about Sunjin?* Surely he hadn't reported Julie? No…she couldn't believe that. By the time she'd fastened her shirt she knew exactly what to do: leave the build-ing, cross town, intercept Sunjin on his way to work. *Then I'll make a run for it, mix with the rush-hour workers. Then the alarm will go up. Damn it!…I'm never late for work.*

As for Sunjin, she thought, he'd have to decide for himself—make a dash, or tie up those loose ends, leave later in the day. She pulled a casual top out of her wardrobe, a top she wore off-duty, and stuffed it into her bag. She took a piece of paper, wrote the name of her florist, scribbled a list of plants. Ridiculous, but she still added, *Say Jayna sent you.* And left it by the cage. She picked up her bag but returned to the list. With pen on paper, poised to offer a final few words to Harry and Lucas, she hesitated—one second, two seconds, three seconds, four seconds—and gave up. Her pen left a faint dot of ink, a mark of her indecision. She added two similar dots along-side and hoped her friends would recognize this failed attempt to explain.

She opened the door by a crack and listened…A few sounds, distant clattery noises reduced by each intervening wall and floor to a less peaky sound but nevertheless telling her that preparations were underway for breakfast. Lights-up in twenty-five minutes, breakfast starting in forty-five. She could slip out now without meeting any residents. And so, with a few steps along her corridor and her descent of the side staircase, a short walk across the ground floor hallway and down the side-entrance steps, she put rest-station life behind her. How many times had she made this journey from her room to the pavement? Yet today, simply because she made the journey earlier than normal, because her teeth were unbrushed, she was not simply leaving but running away.

The street seemed unfamiliar because of the hour. She welcomed the cool, fresh air that helped her to focus, kept her alert. She heard the gasping breaths of a jogger pounding the opposite pavement. A single piece of paper jumped and stumbled along the gutter in the early breeze. She conjured a mantra to keep her pulse steady—*walking this street, breathing this air, walking this street, breathing this air, walking this street*—which forced an easy pace that somehow shielded her as she crossed Oxford Street and descended the steps to the canal.

Time to kill before Sunjin left his residence. She waited awhile under the canal bridge. No one was around as yet to see her loitering but the canal path would become busy over the next half an hour. Jayna looked up at the underside of the red and green painted steelwork. No wonder people wanted to build these things; they would sit in the world for ever. If she could start over…she'd spend more time along these lovely canals, feed the koi rather than pigeons.

A speck of a person in the distance. She waited until the figure came closer and then she set off towards the intersections of canals and rail bridges on the western edge of the commercial district. With no one in sight she stepped into the deepest shadow and stood with her back against a colossal steel column, one of many carrying shuttle lines from the north and west deep into the city's heart. The early shuttles thundered overhead. She made no conscious decision to break cover but impatience got the upper hand and she stepped out from behind the column and walked on. After several erratically timed stop-starts she arrived at the canal steps just two blocks from Sunjin's residence.

From the top of the steps, she walked one block closer and positioned herself by an office entrance as though waiting to meet someone before going into work. All she could do was wait. Sixteen minutes later, far longer than she had expected, Sunjin left his residence and walked along Jayna's side of the street. She turned her back. As he passed she followed and, a half-stride behind him, she spoke: "Don't turn round Sunjin, it's me." And she rattled out the story. She moved ahead of him and he spoke: "We've both got to run, not together though. I'll give you a head start. Good luck."

Jayna peeled off at the next junction and set her route to the Southern Terminus. She realized she looked far too corporate. *I need to look like an office cleaner returning home to the enclaves.* So she took off her jacket and carried it over her arm. It wasn't enough. *I need to appear less symmetrical, more casual.* She forced herself to slow down and let her head loll untidily from side-to-side. One hand in her pocket.

Harry and Lucas, she thought, must have worried about Julie's absence at breakfast, not about *hers*. They would assume she'd rushed out for a breakfast meeting at Mayhew's.

The main streets were busier though the pace was less than frenetic. These were the early risers, the early starters, who walked with longer and slower strides. She knew how Dave would describe them: sad bastards. And one of those sad bastards might be a Mayhew McCline employee so she had to be vigilant. How would she explain herself? Her legs felt weak. *It's no big deal. It's simple: merge with the enclave night-workers heading back. Plenty of shuttles—check the concourse monitors and find the platform.*

But she still looked too tidy so she slipped into the foyer of the university's mathematics building, took her crumpled jumper out of her bag and replaced it with her jacket. She slung the jumper untidily around her shoulders. Off she went again. Into a slow stride, she passed the university park, under the whitebeam, across the cobbles, over the paving slabs, into the terminus piazza. She weaved through the rivulets of workers arriving from the suburbs and enclaves, and cast glances to each side. All fine. A normal day. Everyone looked past her. Again, she glanced left and right. And the closer she came to the concourse the less conspicuous she felt—she was just one figure in a mass of people funneling through the station's entrance.

She strode across the concourse.

It was then, as she stopped to check the overhead monitors— she registered a stuttering in her peripheral vision. A surge inside— adrenalin? She looked left and right but couldn't be sure. She lifted her heavy face to the monitors: **Departures, Arrivals.** Her legs weakened. She didn't look around but waited for a further sign. It came. Two figures both took a step towards her from left and right. She looked again at the monitors. Two shuttles to Enclave W8, both **Delayed.** If Jayna had pointed her hands at the two men she would have formed an angle of 160 degrees. Next shuttle departure—to anywhere—seven minutes.

They won't shout out, she thought. *They're not police. They probably won't chase.*

Arrivals: Platform 11, Shuttle Approaching.

The man to her right, just seven meters away, stepped forward. "Jayna!"

She looked at the monitor. **Shuttle Approaching.**

She ran, bisecting an imaginary arc between the two men. She deviated, sharply, towards platform eleven, a hundred or so meters away. And through the crowds she saw the distant twinkling of shuttle headlights approaching the far end of the station. Too far? The men didn't shout. She tried to glance backwards but the world shook; she'd never run before. She deviated again, turned onto the platform, and sprinted. And the calculations began: the length of the platform, the current speed of the shuttle, its rate of deceleration, her own terminal speed, their combined speed at impact.

The shuttle headlights blazed down the track. She could not run any faster. And just three words in her mind: *end it here.* The men shouted. Her head back, she lengthened her stride. The shuttle still charged down. She anticipated the thud, the end. But her left foot snagged and the pain in her ribs abated too soon. Her brief flight ended as she crashed, arms out, to the paved edge of the platform. The shuttle belted past.

The men reached her before the shuttle came to a halt. The passengers alighted, unaware of the near miss; unaware that for the first time in many years, someone had attempted to end their life in such an arcane manner. Maybe one or two commuters did register, momentarily, the three figures who stood in a huddle: one woman, her head dropped forward, supported by two men. But the working day lay ahead. The workers pressed on and just one person within the herd tripped on a marginally raised manhole cover.

Indeed, the incident caused no ripple of disruption in the routine of the Southern Terminus. No one incurred any delay and sixteen minutes after Jayna's fall, when Dave crossed the concourse, everything appeared as normal.

EPILOGUE 1

The early sun floods the gentle slopes facing east and shifts the true colors of the ripening fruit towards a false warmth. When the dew has dried, they will check the fruit and pick the largest specimens. This is part of the plan: to increase revenue from their small farm by picking fruit only when it reaches full maturity. It seems an obvious strategy but plenty smallholders have not figured this out. They opt for smaller profits today rather than larger profits deferred.

It shouldn't take a genius.

There's no need to be up so early but Dave rises at this hour most days for two simple pleasures: the pleasure of wearing a heavy jacket when the sun is bright but the air still cool, and the greater pleasure of pacing the orchards alone—no one hears what he hears or sees what he sees. He's the only witness; the world is his.

A narrow road winds high along the sheltered valley. On Wednesday, he will travel along this road on his scooter-cart taking twenty-four boxes of assorted citrus to the farm cooperative. On Thursday, the fruit will be displayed in the better suburban delicatessens. Maybe next season, he thinks, he will find another way to sell. But for now, it's best to stick with the normal channel. As Sunjin says, they don't want to look too smart. *Yeah, that makes sense.*

He sits on the wooden seat he knocked together from scrap soon after they arrived at the farm. From here, he looks down the valley across the top of his citrus trees; smatterings of orange and yellow against deep green.

He still thinks of Sunjin as "Sunjin" though his friend lives easily with his new name. And he smiles. Sunjin sees the whole subterfuge as some sort of professional challenge. "I like to imagine," he once explained, "that I've gone covert. You know, police officers went undercover for years. And, if they could hack it, so can I. It's called deep cover."

He'll never lose the lingo, Dave thinks. Even so, he is quietly impressed. Sunjin, the farmhand: in character, he never speaks unless spoken to, stays in the background on the rare occasions when someone visits—a utility worker or their neighbor who likes to pass the time of day by sharing the minutiae of their endeavors. Dave sidesteps these social encounters as best he can. In any case, he needs no advice. He sometimes looks at Sunjin and sees a man whose every waking thought is devoted to these five acres as though he's never known or wished for any other life.

But Dave can't let go in the same way.

During these quiet times, as he looks over the orchards, he gnaws at old bones. It's a habit he can't drop yet it brings no satisfaction. He recalls conversations and tries to edit them with hindsight; tries to force a different emphasis onto the words he spoke back then, words he now re-enacts, slightly amended. Three years have passed and he still tries to make the words come out differently. *I should have...I could have said...*

And, all the while, his eyes flick to the winding road and a mental image is repeatedly triggered. He imagines—though he never formulates or captures any words inside his head—a figure, walking along a section of the road that's beyond his view. The figure must surely emerge; he wills it to happen.

He feels good in many ways. He's beaten the system. But he feels cheated—it could be so much better.

Dave knows the Constructor picked her up at the terminus. The whole office knew the day it happened. "It was total fucking mayhem," he told Sunjin later. Everyone heard Olivia and Benjamin; they screamed blue murder at the Constructor. But there was no getting her back, the small print made sure of that. He looks back and struggles to remember any detail from the first days. He was stupefied, dumb, numb. And though no one questioned him, about anything, he broke into sweats. He hid himself away in Archives and all he can recall now is an acrid smell that wafted upwards from his sticking shirt, and a sense of stasis.

On the Saturday after her disappearance, he traveled to Enclave W8, to the safe house where he found Sunjin. And on the next three Saturdays, he returned with provisions. With each visit they refined a plan.

At first, their plan was simple. Sunjin would disappear for a few months among the migrant workers, just to get out of sight. He couldn't hang around the safe house indefinitely. Neighbors might have become curious. They talked about the money stashed in bank accounts, share certificates, the bio data for false identities, which Sunjin had grabbed before scarpering. But Sunjin had insisted: no touching the money, perhaps not for a long time.

Sometime around his second or third visit, Dave can't quite remember now, he mentioned to Sunjin about the walk down Clothing Street, the things she'd said later in his flat. They returned time and time again to these shards of conversation. "But she only said it in passing," Dave had said. Sunjin was sure they should act on her few remarks. She was, after all, the guru on such matters. So, when Dave eventually found a buyer for the Wiener Werkstätte brooch (it was, as she'd scribbled on the scrap of paper, a Josef Hoffmann design) their ideas had coalesced. A trader's license it would be. And the nature of Dave's trading was also clear. For her words were incised from constant use: *People don't need to buy books but they do need to buy food.*

Finally, Dave provoked an argument with Hester. He was out the same day.

We've done well.

He hears the satisfying, wholesome sounds of empty wooden boxes being stacked over on the far side of the farmhouse. Sunjin's day has started. Soon the irrigation system will kick in and he'll start his morning rounds. He'll meticulously check any suspect nozzles, look for any leaks, before he takes his breakfast. Sunjin, the sleuth, turned farmhand. Dave laughs quietly, under his breath, at the mental image of Sunjin darting around the orchards, a long-haired, manic preacher who makes the trees sing to his tune. And Dave remembers a conversation he had with Sunjin two weeks ago, when they'd sat together replacing damaged slats in some of those fruit boxes: "Are you all right doing this, Sunjin?"

"I'm making a fair job of it."

"No, I don't mean that. Are you bored doing this sort of thing?"

"It's all part of the process."

"But are you enjoying it?"

"Yes, I like the process."

"What?"

Sunjin had explained, patiently: "I like the small tasks because I know how they fit within the overall venture. It's the attention to detail that makes the whole operation work smoothly. How will the cooperative regard you, Dave, if you turn up with battered boxes? I'll tell you. They'll think you're a loser. And what's the point of us running our farm with such care if a protruding nail scratches a single fruit? One protruding nail in, say, 30 per cent of our boxes would make a serious dent in our gross profit. It's all a question of detail. Our margins are too slender to throw money away simply through a lack of rigor."

"Suppose so."

"I know so. I've seen it with my own eyes."

Which indeed he had.

When Dave bought his license to work as a fruit vendor, Sunjin became an itinerant and worked among the major citrus groves and smallholdings, west of the enclaves. He moved from farm to farm and slept in huts or under canvas, whatever the owners cared to provide. While Dave learned how to sell, Sunjin learned how to farm. He was on a mission: to learn, observe, absorb everything—varieties, planting schemes, root stocks, grafting, how to prune, when to cut back, how to irrigate, when to water, when not to water, when to pick, when not to pick. He became a collector of ideas and good practice; one idea from here, another from there. He learnt from the bad farmers and the good farmers alike—all the time he collected evidence for later prosecution. When they met as planned, eighteen months later, Dave barely recognized him with his matted hair, tautened physique, and sun-blackened skin.

Dave stirs from his morning vigil and makes his way up the slope to complete his circuit. *Who would have thought…?* These words have become wind chimes and they hang from all the trees. He hears them day in, day out.

Sunjin continued as a laborer for a further six months after meeting Dave. By then they had accumulated a small but significant pot of savings and, more to the point, Dave had operated his stall long enough to justify, to the outside world, an elevation in his circumstances. He took out a loan and augmented their savings with a modest cash withdrawal from one of their many fraudulent nest eggs. Dave acted on Sunjin's advice and bought a neglected smallholding of mixed citrus and avocado. And the new double-act began: Dave the moderately successful entrepreneur and his one farmhand, a farmhand who knew how to turn around a failing enterprise.

At the very least, the farm will become a front, to mask their earnings from elsewhere.

Dave reaches the highest irrigation block on his circuit and smacks the top of a stumped avocado. It grieved him when they moved to the farm that, straight off, Sunjin had decided to cut half the avocado trees down to one-meter stumps. "They're overcrowded, too tall for efficient harvesting." He now sees the sense in it. They will start to produce after four or five years and, at that point, the rest of the avocado grove will be stumped. One day, they will reap the benefit of a surgical approach. But it still seems brutal.

By the side of the farmhouse door stands a specimen Jamaican tangelo; its boughs hang over the kitchen yard. To Dave's mind, there's no taste like the Ugli fruit of this tree. Its tangy sweetness belies an ill-favored appearance. He sits outside many evenings and stares up into the canopy, convinced he can see the unlovely fruits grow.

This is their tree. They take the best of the harvest for their own table. It's their only extravagance. And Dave loves this tangelo tree most of all on a morning such as this when a perfectly ripe fruit hangs within easy reach just over the kitchen door.

He looks across to the higher slopes. Sunjin is making his way into the far orchard. Dave shouts, "Breakfast in twenty!" He pulls the fruit. And Sunjin, without turning, raises his hand.

EPILOGUE 2

"**With respect, Beatrice, how many times** in the past six months has anyone referred to any of these books in relation to a billable job?"

"That's not the point."

"In the last year? Two years? I've been here nearly four years and I can only recall eight occasions."

"It's still not the point."

"But I believe it is." Hannah feels she must stand up to this resolute octogenarian. "You see, if we auction the most valuable—the ancient documents and the first editions—and then donate the rest to whoever you like—The Law Society, The Inns of Court Library—we'd raise a great deal of money that we could invest in more extensive digitized access. Our fee-earners need the very best. And, we could free up shelf space for more pertinent documentation that's currently festering in storage." *Mistake. I've given two reasons instead of one. Each reason will undermine the validity of the other.*

"I can't believe we're talking about shelf space."

I walked into that one. Hannah is aware that she's operating slightly under par; not tired, as such, but her nights have become heavy with dreams. How long has it been going on? Four, five weeks? At least. Now she comes to think of it, her first bad dream occurred seven weeks ago. There was a gap of two weeks before it returned and since then it has reoccurred with ever-greater frequency; most nights now. These nocturnal spins leave her slightly disoriented and off-center. It's as if the color of her dreams tinges her waking hours. She wonders if she has experienced a troubling conversation that's still lurking just beneath her consciousness. That's exactly how it feels: as though there's unfinished business, something left in abeyance.

"I know my attitude to the library may seem callous, Beatrice—"

"It's an outrageous suggestion you're making. Surely you see that," interrupts the senior partner, evidently taken aback by the degree of Hannah's insensitivity on the matter.

"It's my job to make sure the knowledge management system in this law firm is second to none. We need to guarantee speed to give us a strong competitive edge."

"On the other hand, think about this, Hannah. We are one of the oldest established firms in the City. It's an important differentiator. That's why we use this room for key-client meetings." She waves her walking stick at the perfectly arranged, perfectly categorized tomes. "These old books say to our clients 'We've been here a long time. We've seen it all before. There's nothing we can't handle.' Or do you suggest we sell the collection and put fake books in their place?"

"Of course not."

"Our clients love this room and they don't give a damn about our problems with shelf space."

Hannah's back stiffens. Strong language bothers her somehow. When anyone in the office swears she instinctively prickles. She asked her friends back at the rest station if their colleagues used bad language. No one seemed to share her concern. It's not that she dislikes this form of speech. She just reacts, she feels, more than she ought.

"More than anything else, Beatrice, our clients want fast results. So can we decide here and now to increase my budget, with or without selling off the library?"

"Hannah, the library is not even up for discussion." Nevertheless, Beatrice sags as if defeated. "I just wish you could appreciate…" Her voice trails off as though the conversation is exhausting her.

"Appreciate what?" she says quietly.

"The history of these things."

Hannah raises her eyebrows in reply.

"Have you ever looked at *any* of these books?"

"Well, no. That's surely the point. I haven't needed to."

"But you've noticed, Hannah, that other directors come in here, from time to time, to leaf through old volumes."

"Yes. But it's usually the more…senior directors."

"And do you ever wonder why they come in here?"

"I do. I assume it's one of those things I just can't grasp. It's beyond me."

Beatrice stares hard at her. She knows this woman will accept her rebuff with good grace. But she would still like to help her to understand. "You see, Hannah…it's about a different path to…revelation. How can I say it? A path that's more direct— not quicker, but more direct—by which I mean less mediated. And it's not simply a matter of being old-fashioned, and it's not nostalgia."

"Then what?"

"Well, for one thing, it feels more satisfying…to remember a case in the Law Reports, or to recall something mentioned at a conference, or a reference made years before by a colleague, or to find a judgment in a digital catalogue… The point—" she nods her head in emphasis "—the point is…it's a thrill to know we have the original case report here in the library. To find the specific bound volume, slide it from the shelf, and turn the pages. Your eyes hit the names. You have it, there, in your hands."

"It's the same information, though. And it's slower to access."

"I know." Beatrice stamps the polished wooden floor with her walking stick. "But there's something about finding—" she stamps the floor again "—the book."

Is this what happens in old age, Hannah wonders? *You can't find the words to convey your thoughts. It's in your head but you can't translate the idea into language. If only I could be inside Beatrice's mind at this very moment and see for myself.* Hannah offers a conciliatory smile but she won't give in. "I think you're mistaken, Beatrice. It's pure nostalgia…Let's agree to disagree, shall we?"

Beatrice pushes herself out of the chair and the younger woman steps forward to take her arm. "You can have your bigger budget. But you're not selling our library."

"Fine. Thank you."

"There's one condition. I want you to spend the rest of today in here, Hannah. I want you to look at these books. Touch them. Maybe you'll see things my way if you immerse yourself. I'll make sure you won't be disturbed."

"I have meetings at eleven and two-thirty."

"Internal?"

"Yes."

"Cancel them."

Hannah tilts her head sideways. "Okay then. It's a deal." She opens the tall library doors for her colleague.

"Try to keep in mind—" Beatrice halts on the threshold "—that this library holds many, thousands, of the judicial decisions that make up our common law, and that common law is constantly evolving; the law is a living process and you can touch it here. You can follow the paper-trail, read the views of legal commentators through the decades, the centuries even." She rallies herself, for she won't give up on Hannah. "Look at the Law Reports and the first editions; they're so close, so proximate to the courtrooms of the day—" she leans forward "—you can almost hear the judges, the barristers, speaking; feel them breathing out of the page." But she knows she still hasn't conveyed her feelings. She can't quite get there.

"I promise, Beatrice. I will try."

———

She stands by the leather armchair vacated by Beatrice and surveys the library. The furniture arrangement, she notices, coerces any visitor to sit in solitary contemplation. It's more of a shrine for her older colleagues. She pushes her hands through her hair. There are so many other tasks she could be working on today. But if Beatrice wants her to do this, how can she refuse? And does it matter which books she looks at? No. It can't possibly make any difference.

She slowly paces the perimeter of the library, tracing with her forefinger the shelf at shoulder height. She sighs at the thought of Beatrice's delusion that these books offer a particular pleasure. *All the information in these books is so static. It's so utterly pointless... Maybe I'll go through the motions.* She likes the phrase. It conjures the idea of a physical process, executed on automatic, that serves neither practical nor intellectual purpose. But there's a hint of deception, too, which she's not entirely sure about. *A few quiet hours in here, a few hours of analysis, might help to clear my head, help me work out what's wrong. I want to pinpoint this feeling of unfinished business, whatever it is.* She pulls a book, not bothering to read the spine, and returns to the armchair. *Should I report my nightmares to the Constructor? Or wait?*

The book lies in her lap.

After all, the dreams may stop as suddenly as they began. She places her fingertips together and rubs her forefingers against her chin. Sitting in silence, she stares through the library's high arched windows at the neighboring glass-fronted towers and watches the minor movements of people in their offices. All doing their bit, unaware of her gaze. And it seems incongruous to her that, here, in the heart of the capital's commercial district she finds herself effectively task-free, completely idle. Or, at least, she regards looking at old books as a fairly idle way of passing a whole day.

So. The nightmares. The first thing that concerns her is that she can't get a fix on them. There are no images, no specific thoughts, no narratives. She wakes the same way most mornings now, with her heart pounding and a thick sheet of sweat coating her skin. That is, she wakes in fear. She knows such a strong emotion should be alien to her but she doesn't feel inclined to broadcast her problem. Thus, a new precaution has entered her routine. She keeps a towel on her bed overnight and when jolted out of her dream into the very real surroundings of her quarters she sits up and dries herself. And in the morning, she throws back the sheets, allowing them to dry before she leaves for work, and before the rest-station domestics make their rounds.

Two nights ago, she experienced a new development. As she fell towards sleep, she felt a tension in the muscles of her lower arms and she knew, most surely, that this sensation presaged the onset of a nightmare. She forced herself, on the cusp of sleep, to leave her bed and pace the small room. Then she washed herself down with a wet cloth and made sure she was fully awake before she dared attempt sleep once more.

The second thing that perplexes Hannah arises from her private research conducted in her own time—research, that is, on sleep dysfunction. This is the real reason she's in no hurry to contact her Constructor. It appears, according to medical papers—or, more specifically, mental health papers—that there's a link between the frequency of nightmares and suicidality. There's no consensus on whether this is a causal relationship but the statistics are striking. And the nightmare link seems to correlate not only for people with a current propensity for suicide but also for people who are previous suicide attempters. Which makes no sense to her as far as her own circumstances are concerned. It must be a red herring.

Maybe it's simpler than that. Maybe there's something causing me stress that I've failed to recognize; something that isn't too serious but is sufficient to unbalance my particular psyche. It could be a recognized phenomenon. The Constructor may already hold an easy remedy.

She stares out at the office workers and wonders if they, too, absorb stresses in their daily routines, unaware of the physical manifestations that may follow. Quite likely. They probably have a lower stress threshold. And, naturally, her own tasks are well within her capabilities whereas they must find themselves out of their depth occasionally.

She explores the book in her lap without consciously making the decision to do so. It's a tactile curiosity that compels her hands to test the book's surfaces: the textured leather binding, the embossed lettering, and the smooth-edged pages. Her fingers investigate these edges, finding the page marker—a burgundy-red ribbon, which she instinctively pulls sideways and then up, slipping her thumb between the pages. Her eyes, however, are fixed ahead. An office worker is waving, she assumes, to attract a colleague's attention and she scans across. But, before she can find the recipient of the wave, Hannah is distracted by…it's like a tapping on the center of her forehead. Her focus retracts as she notices for the first time that the library has a fustiness. This realization only dawns now because the book in her lap acts as an amplifier. She finds the imprint. This book has remained closed, she reckons, for over one hundred years. *Ridiculous waste of space.* The book creaks as though ready to snap as she spreads open the pages. She registers the archaic form of legal reporting, so resistant to change: the emboldened and capitalized names of judges—surname, initials, full-stop, colon; the margin numberings—H1, H2, H3— set beneath the headings, Introduction, Facts, Held; and margin numberings—1, 2, 3, 4—set beneath the Judgment. She flicks the pages and lifts the open book to her face with both hands, in a movement that seems as ancient as the book itself. She inhales.

It's a specific, almost recognizable smell. It makes her scramble to place a marker.

She thinks, feels…what? She lifts the book closer. The tip of her nose touches the ink. The smell hits her now—a slap! She's rooted in the armchair. And there she stays for minutes. She breathes steadily and waits for a spark, a word or thought, an image. She chases barely formed feelings, hunts for an association, for the source, and tries to transport herself to another place far from here. And, at last, she sees something.

A clear sky and a lazy flapping sheet; it's pink.

She stands, drops the book to the floor, walks to the nearest shelf and pulls *Chitty on Contracts* by the top of its spine. It's tightly wedged and the spine tears. Hannah opens the book at random, page 1095, chapter twenty-three, *Discharge by Frustration*, and she inhales, deeply, before pushing it back atop its sequenced partner editions. She tears another spine, opens and inhales, drops the book and takes another, testing again. And another, grasping pages, dropping more books until she's halfway around the library.

How easily a room surrenders its order and harmony.

She walks over to the window, stares without seeing, clutching a handful of torn pages. What is she trying to uncover—a thought, an idea, something familiar that she's misplaced? It can't be that, surely. She never forgets anything; she knows the sum total of her life as well as her life's every incremental progression.

A siren is just audible twenty-three floors below her and she sees an ambulance crossing Blackfriars Bridge with a police escort; not much work for the constabulary these days. And, as the two flashing vehicles swerve around a recycling truck, she maps—for she can't help herself—the one-way system at the southern end of the bridge and determines the shortest route to Guy's Hospital. But in her subconscious, other thoughts are meandering in loops of great magnitude. She stares across at the office workers—doing their best, trying so hard.

The ambulance will be there. She feels relieved for someone she's never met. Meanwhile, the deep meandering thoughts reach a precipice and, in their free-fall, Hannah gleans and grasps a moment of clarity. *I'm not trying to remember—It's the other way around. My memory is trying to find me.* She raises the torn pages to her face. *A blue sky, a pink sheet. I can figure this out.*

ACKNOWLEDGEMENTS

I have the pleasure of thanking individual members of the Charnock Family (Garry, Adam, and Robert), Andrew Fletcher, Roy and Roberta Nurmi, Basheera Khan, Fiona Curran, Mike Lemmy, and Margaret Garman. I am also grateful to my editor David Pomerico and all the team at 47North for their support and enthusiasm.

Several non-fiction books provided useful background material for *A Calculated Life*. These included Antonio Damasio's *Looking for Spinoza—Joy, Sorrow and the Feeling Brain*, Simon Singh's *Fermat's Last Theorem*, and Nassim Nicholas Taleb's *The Black Swan—The Impact of the Highly Improbable*. In the chapter *Confirmation Shmonfirmation!* in Taleb's book, he suggests that the nature of human instinct was formed in primitive environments and is ill-suited to the modern world.

Some of the ideas I explore in this novel came to my attention in Ray Kurzweil's *The Age of Spiritual Machines*. In this book, Kurzweil predicted the future for neural implants.

I am grateful for a conversation I had with Kevin Warwick at the University of Reading. He later wrote *I, Cyborg*—the story of how he became the guinea pig for his own implantation research.

On a more specific subject, the earliest known writing that refers to citrus fruit is contained in the book *Yu Kung* or *Tribute of Yu*. Emperor Ta Yu reigned from 2205 to 2197 BC. I came across this fact in *History and Development of the Citrus Industry* by Herbert John Webber (revised by Walter Reuther and Harry W. Lawton).

I also thank the many contributors to online forums for sharing their knowledge about citrus growing, bee keeping, and stick insects.

Recumbent Figure of Jesse, which I refer to as *Jesse Recumbent*, was exhibited at Tate Britain's *Image and Idol: Medieval Sculpture* in 2001. It was sculpted from oak in the late fifteenth century and was loaned by St Mary's Priory Church, Abergavenny, Wales.

I may have occasionally misinterpreted my research sources or added embellishments for fictional purposes. For the former, I apologize.

ABOUT THE AUTHOR

Garry Charnock © 2012

Anne Charnock's writing career began in journalism; her articles appeared in *The Guardian, New Scientist, International Herald Tribune,* and *Geographical.* She was educated at the University of East Anglia, where she studied environmental sciences, and at The Manchester School of Art. She travelled widely as a foreign correspondent and spent a year trekking through Egypt, Sudan, and Kenya.

In her fine art practice she tried to answer the questions *What is it to be human? What is it to be a machine?* and ultimately she decided to write fiction as another route to finding answers.

Anne is an active blogger and reviews fiction for the online magazine *Strange Horizons.* She contributes exhibition reviews and book recommendations to *The Huffington Post.* She splits her time between London and Chester and, whenever possible, she and her husband Garry take off in their little campervan (unless one of their two sons has borrowed it), traveling as far as the Anti-Atlas Mountains in southern Morocco.

http://www.annecharnock.com
http://www.twitter.com/annecharnock

Printed in Great Britain
by Amazon